# Gone Wild

# Gone Wild

### Jodi Lundgren

JAMES LORIMER & COMPANY LTD., PUBLISHERS
TORONTO

James Lorimer & Company Ltd., Publishers acknowledges the support of the Ontario Arts Council. We acknowledge the support of the Canada Council for the Arts which last year invested $24.3 million in writing and publishing throughout Canada. We acknowledge the Government of Ontario through the Ontario Media Development Corporation's Ontario Book Initiative.

Cover design: Meredith Bangay
Cover images: Brandi Pringle (background), Shutterstock (characters)

Library and Archives Canada Cataloguing in Publication available

ISBN 978-1-4594-0989-7

James Lorimer & Company Ltd.,
Publishers
317 Adelaide Street West, Suite 1002
Toronto, ON, Canada
M5V 1P9
www.lorimer.ca

Distributed in the United States by:
Lerner Publishing Group
1251 Washington Ave N
Minneapolis, MN, USA
55401

Printed and bound in Canada.
Manufactured by Friesens Corporation in Altona, Manitoba, Canada in January 2016.
Job #220058

# Prologue

*Neck-deep in a cold ocean bay, two teenaged runaways struggle toward shore. The girl is weighed down by a heavy pack that's absorbing more water by the second. She needs to shuck it off to keep from drowning. The boy is trying to help her, but he might not be strong enough.*

*No one else in the coastal park sees what is happening. Even if a ranger happened to be near, he'd be patrolling the woods — clearing the windfall from a late spring storm or checking back-country camping permits. It isn't his job to rescue backpackers from the water. It's their job to keep out of it.*

*At least the tide is helping. Each new wave tosses the teens a little closer to the rocky beach. Their heads bob above the water. Both have brown-black hair — the colour of wet soil.*

# CHAPTER 1

# Seth: Letter

Seth drags his feet as he walks home from school. Traffic whizzes past on the four-lane road. Nothing's more depressing than this cement sidewalk, except maybe the skinny trees that poke up beside it every twelve feet. Even though it's June, the trees have hardly any leaves. The exhaust fumes must be killing them.

It's three o'clock on a Friday, and he's got nowhere to go. For the past few months, he's been hanging out with the stoners after school. He's usually too broke to chip in, so he doesn't toke much. But they're pretty chill, and it's better than being alone.

Things changed last week when he had to stay after school to meet with the counsellor. Seth tried to explain to her that his failing grades didn't mean he had problems at home. He was just lazy with a side-order of dumb. The counsellor didn't laugh. Instead, she recommended tutoring for his school-work, along with counselling for his low self-esteem. *Like that's going to happen.*

While Seth was trapped in the counsellor's office, his

friends were getting busted. They were suspended for a week, and since then, he hasn't heard from any of them. They probably grudge him for his lucky escape. No big deal. He's never stuck with a group of friends past the end of the school year, anyway. It's better not to push his luck.

He turns off the four-lane road onto a narrower street lined with apartment blocks. The street dead-ends at a park. He takes a shortcut across it, passing the off-leash area where a bunch of dogs are chasing each other and fetching balls. There's a pang in his chest. *God, I miss him.* Walking his dog Patches, a floppy-eared Jack Russell, used to give Seth a reason to go home after school. Getting welcomed with yips and tail-wags always cheered him up. But a few months ago, his dad came back and took Patches. "He can ride in the front seat of my truck and run around at every rest stop," his dad said. "It's not fair to leave him cooped up all day." *Fair to who?* Now Seth sees his dog only when he visits his dad every other weekend.

On days like today, all that's waiting for him is an empty apartment or, even worse, his mom's new boyfriend, Bert. *Rhymes with hurt.* Supposedly, Bert works two weeks on, two weeks off. All Seth knows for sure is that he hangs around a lot.

As Seth gets closer to home, Bert's truck comes into view, jacked up on the curb as usual. He's the kind of guy who thinks parking with all your tires on the road is for pussies. He likes 4X4ing, ATVing, and hunting, or that's what he says. Mostly, he cracks one beer after another in front of the TV. Hockey, UFC, and one time a porno that Seth walked in on by accident. Bert swore and Seth backed out of the room. The sound of a zipper made Seth wince. Bert didn't even try to joke about it later. After that, Bert seemed to have it in for him even more than before.

Seth considers doubling back and waiting in the park until

his mom comes home at five. But Bert has seen him. He opens the sliding glass door, and Seth braces himself.

Bert waves a white envelope in his hand. "Mr. Death!" That's the charming nickname he's come up with for Seth. "You got mail!"

Seth's stomach drops to somewhere between his crotch and the ground. He's had one last hope to keep him going. He's been waiting for a letter that could change everything. His heart pounds so fast that he trembles all over.

He takes a flying run at the envelope, but Bert lifts it over his head and holds up his other hand like a stop sign. "BC Adoption Registry?" Bert says. "Does your mom know about this?"

When Seth wrote the letter months ago, Bert wasn't in the picture. Seth used to pick up the mail every single day. His mom wasn't ever supposed to hear about this.

Bert shifts his weight, blocking the entrance to the sliding glass door. Seth wishes he could attack, but Bert is taller and heavier. He likes to wrestle Seth to the ground, kneel across his chest, and make him beg for mercy. The first time Bert did it, Seth didn't beg, and Bert lowered his weight onto Seth's chest until his lungs were crushed and he was choking for air. The bastard could've killed him. Nothing that bad had happened since foster care.

Seth and his half-brother Keith got taken away from their dad when Seth was only two. Keith used to beat Seth up, and since he was five years older, the fights were never fair. The worst one happened when their birth dad finally arranged a visit and then didn't show. "Me and Dad were doing just fine until you came along!" Keith pushed Seth to the ground and then kicked him over and over, saying foster care was all Seth's fault.

Seth stares over Bert's head at the envelope, and the inside of his chest burns with rage. He twists away and heads for the front entrance to the apartment block. He's got to get that envelope.

He's sweating as he unlocks the door to the lobby. He slips inside, rounds the corner, and lets himself into the apartment. The TV blares in the living room. Has Bert forgotten about him already? Seth kicks off his shoes but keeps his jacket on. He doesn't even take off his empty backpack. He edges into the kitchen in his stocking feet. He slides across the linoleum floor into the dining nook. From here he can see the back of Bert's head as he slouches on the sofa, watching a game. The white envelope lies on the coffee table in front of him.

Seth inches forward. Bert yells at the TV, and the crowd cheers. Seth dives across the arm of the couch and snatches the envelope. He tenses, waiting for Bert to grasp his arm, but nothing happens. He loses his balance and stumbles. Bert chuckles. "Easy does it, kid."

Seth spins around. Bert's smiling. The only time he smiles is when he's got the upper hand. Seth flips the envelope over. The back flap has lifted up. Bert must have steamed it open.

"Read it and weep, buddy."

The blood drains out of Seth's face. *That asshole read my mail? And what does he mean by "read it and weep"?* Seth's whole body is shaking. He makes a dash for the front hall, shoves his feet into his shoes, and flings open the door. He rounds the corner and bursts through the main entrance. He keeps running to the park at the end of the street. Shaking and gasping for breath, he slumps on a bench. A crow perched on the lip of a nearby garbage can flaps its wings and lifts into the air. It lands on the ground a few feet away.

Seth tugs the letter out of the envelope and unfolds the paper.

*Your request to contact your birth mother has been received. We regret to inform you that adoptees under the age of nineteen are not eligible to access the adoption registry. We encourage you to renew your request when you reach adulthood.*

*We understand how disappointing this response can be for young adoptees. We recommend the following teen counselling agencies . . .*

Seth can't hold it together anymore. He balls up the envelope and throws it on the ground. "God damn it!" For a whole year, this dream has been the only thing keeping him going. Listening to his parents fight, losing Patches, getting tortured by Rhymes-with-hurt, being haunted by memories of foster care and Keith — he's survived all of it by dreaming of his birth mom. In a few days he's turning sixteen. This year, he was hoping to talk to her for the first time and hear her say, *Happy birthday. I always think of you on this day.*

In his daydreams, she has warm eyes. She's young-looking and pretty, with long, dark hair. She says, *I've never stopped loving you. Maybe you can stay with me for a while, so we can get to know each other.* They walk along the beach with her dog. He just knows she has one. And somehow he gets Patches back, and the two dogs run free on the sand.

All Seth knows about his birth mom is that she couldn't take care of him. She was only sixteen when he was born. He wishes he could at least see pictures of her and his biological dad, so he could know which one he takes after. In his memories, his half-brother Keith is blue-eyed and pale with sandy hair. Seth, with his dark hair, hazel eyes, and light brown skin, doesn't look anything like him.

The crow hops closer and eyes the crumpled envelope. Seth wipes the cuff of his long-sleeved t-shirt under his nose. His birth mom has probably tried to contact the government agency, too. She must be counting the months until he's old enough. *Why are they making us wait?* He lifts his head. A Canada Post mailbox sits on the curb, fire engine red. He jumps up and charges at it, butting it with his chest, and then his shoulders, as he tries to knock it over. "Screw you, government!" Hollow thuds echo from inside the box, but it's bolted to the ground and doesn't budge.

He straightens up, his body throbbing where he banged the box. On the ground nearby, the crow pecks the crumpled envelope with its beak. It stabs at it a few times, then hops back up to the lip of the garbage can.

When Seth's mom gets home, Bert will tell her about the letter. She'll be upset that Seth wrote to the agency without telling her. She'll either be mad: "You think she would have treated you better than me? Well, you're wrong!" Or sad: "Seth, I've looked after you like my own boy all these years. Why haven't I been enough for you? It's because of the divorce, isn't it?"

Either way, it will be all about her. Seth can't go back there tonight.

He has a key to his dad's place, but the deal is that Seth visits every second weekend. Besides, his dad won't be back from the Calgary run for a couple of days. His dad's chain-smoking roommate will be there, clouding up the place. Patches won't.

*Where the hell am I supposed to go?*

# CHAPTER 2

# Brooke: Late

It's around four o'clock when Brooke pulls into the driveway of the suburban house where she lives with her parents. She turns off the engine and hides the pile of resumes in her bag. She didn't waste her time this afternoon tromping from one coffee shop to another, asking to speak to the manager. No one gets hired that way anymore — but try telling that to her mom.

She pauses on the doorstep. In the driveway, the engine of her twenty-year-old Toyota ticks as it cools down beside her mother's grey sedan. Brooke takes a breath and turns the door handle, hoping she can slip in and make a beeline for her room.

Before she can even shrug off her jacket, her mom looms in the entryway. She's wearing a grey t-shirt and sweatpants, her housecleaning outfit. She plants her feet and folds her arms. "The doctor's office called to schedule your annual check-up."

Brooke bends to unlace her shoes. She knows better than to kick them off and get a lecture about scuff marks.

"Call them back right away, will you? The office is only open 'til four-thirty."

Brooke stands up. Her mom's reddish hair is swept back off her face in a hairband. Freckles stand out on her fair skin, which burns so easily that she avoids the sun. Brooke's glad that she inherited her dad's brunet colouring. Tanning well helps when you love the outdoors. "What's the rush?"

Her mom bends to line up Brooke's shoes perpendicular to the rest of the row. "You should follow up right away. Letting things slide is a bad habit, and no employer will appreciate it."

Brooke brushes past her mother. "Fine." Could she *be* any more controlling?

Her mom follows her into the kitchen. "How is the job search going, anyway?"

Brooke rummages through the cupboards for a snack. All she finds are rice cakes. The plain kind. She opens the fridge and grabs a Fuji apple. No need to wash it because her mom has already done that. Probably three times. Brooke rips into it with her teeth.

Her mom wipes the counter and wrings out the cloth while Brooke chews and swallows. "Did you check with your boss from last summer?"

Brooke holds the apple at her side, pinching it between thumb and forefinger. Ever since she finished her last provincial exam two weeks ago, her mom hasn't quit nagging her. "I told you. Claudia wanted me to stay on during the school year. You didn't want me to. Claudia had to hire someone else, and now she *can't* give me my job back."

Her mom frowns. "I just thought you should focus on school during grade twelve. It's such an important year. I didn't know you were going to throw away your chance to go to university!"

Brooke tightens her grip on the apple. A bubble of anger

14

swells inside her rib cage. Hurling the apple at her mom crosses her mind. She blinks hard to erase the image. "I didn't throw it away. I've got the grades I need to get in."

Her mom's eyebrows pull together, making a deep crease. "Then why won't you go into nursing like your sister? The employment rate for nursing graduates is over ninety percent." According to her mother, Brooke's older sister, Deanna, does everything right. She has disappointed their mother only once: by moving out to go to university when she could have kept living at home. Sometimes Brooke thinks she must have been switched at birth and sent home with the wrong family. Somewhere out there is a laid-back mother who should have been the one to raise her. "I don't want to be a nurse." Brooke shakes her head. "I'm not Deanna."

Her mom scowls. "I don't know *who* you are, ever since Adam came along."

Brooke chomps such a big piece of apple that it takes all her concentration to chew without opening her mouth.

"That boy has been a bad influence on you. I saw it coming from the minute he showed up on a dirt-bike." Her mom puts her hands on her hips, elbows jutting. "And what sort of person gets a tattoo on his neck?"

Brooke isn't in the mood to defend Adam. One of the main reasons she started dating him was to annoy her mother. It worked, but the thrill is wearing off. It's been over a year already.

"And now you want to go into Adventure Studies!"

Brooke clicks her tongue against her teeth. "Adam has nothing to do with that."

As soon as Brooke heard about the Adventure Sport Certificate, she knew her mom would hate the idea. The courses include rock climbing, sea kayaking, and river rafting. She's dying to try them all. She just needs to save up the money.

Her mom grabs a broom. "How can you think those extreme sports are a good idea?"

"They're not really that extreme."

Her mom sweeps the kitchen floor hard and fast. The bristles thump and scrape the linoleum squares. "Two students in that program died in an avalanche last year. What are you, suicidal?"

Brooke swallows. She didn't know her mom had researched the program. "That was a freak accident."

Brooke's mom shakes her head and keeps attacking the floor with her broom. Brooke sighs and trudges out of the kitchen.

"Don't forget to call the doctor! The number's on the fridge."

Brooke turns back to snatch the slip of paper from under a fridge magnet and heads to her room. *Might as well schedule an appointment.* It will give her a reason to leave the house, and that's always a relief.

The receptionist picks up on the second ring. "Dr. Henderson's office."

"This is Brooke Donnelly. My mom said you called?"

"Yes, hello. Just let me get to that screen." She taps a keyboard. "It's time for a full check-up. And now that you're eighteen, Dr. Henderson recommends a pelvic exam."

*A pelvic exam.* Brooke shudders. "Really?" She tries to not to let her voice show how grossed out she feels.

"Yes, I'm afraid so. No one looks forward to them, but it's an important preventative measure that could save your life someday. A little inconvenience is a small price to pay when it comes to your health, don't you think?"

"I guess so."

"To schedule the pelvic exam, we need to know, when did your last period start?"

Brooke wasn't expecting such a personal question. Her face flushes hot. "Um . . . let me check, and I'll call you back."

She unpins the calendar from her bulletin board. A gift from Adam, it's filled with photos of motorbikes. On the day her period starts each month, she scribbles a large round dot. She flips back and finds a dot on May 2. It's now the middle of June.

She places her fingertip on the calendar and traces the weeks, counting out loud. "One — two — three . . ." Six and a half weeks have passed since the start of her last period.

She crosses to the window, leans her forehead on the glass, and massages her temples. This can't be happening.

*Is it the stress of exams? The skipped meals and junk food?*
*Or the night with Adam.*
*Shit.*

When she and Adam first got serious, she could have asked her doctor for the Pill. But her mom would have found out. At least, that's what Brooke was scared of. No way did she want to discuss with her mom the details of what she and Adam did. They did a lot of things, and a condom wasn't usually necessary. But more and more, Adam was craving the kind of sex that required one. Sometimes he even begged her to let him see what it felt like *without* a condom. He promised to control himself, if he could just try it for a minute?

Last month, he finally wore her down.

She turns sideways to the mirror and holds her stomach.

She drops her hand. *It's stupid to think there might be a bump already.* What about her breasts? They've been tender and sore for a while, but that's normal before her period.

Brooke collapses onto the bed. *Now what? A trip to the drugstore for a home pregnancy test?* She can't stand to think of it. There'll be a knowing look on the cashier's face. Maybe a smirk if it's a teenager. A scowl if it's someone older. Can she get Adam to steal one? He knows how to shoplift. He doesn't make a habit of it, but it's one of his so-called "survival skills."

*No. Screw Adam.* She wouldn't be in this mess if it wasn't for him. She'll handle it on her own.

# CHAPTER 3

# Seth: Ride

Seth sinks into a window seat and huddles against the side of the bus, using his backpack as a pillow. The letter from the adoption agency is shoved deep into his coat pocket. For some reason, he couldn't bring himself to rip it up. He just had to get far away before his mom got home at five. He narrows his eyes to slits. It's up to the driver where he goes next. He can shut off his mind for a while.

At Douglas Street, the driver makes everyone get off. Seth stumbles into the sunlight, blinking like he just woke up from a nap. On the wall of the bus shelter, he glances at the map of routes. How far can he get on the city's transit system?

In one direction, a bus will take him to Swartz Bay, where the ferry leaves for the mainland. *Wouldn't it be sweet to escape?* But he's got only five bucks or so. Not enough for the ferry. And anyway, where would he go on the other side?

In the other direction, he could get to Sooke. Further up the west coast, the island gets wilder. Last fall, his science class took a field trip past Sooke to China Beach. They hiked a short section of a wilderness trail through the woods to Mystic Beach. Even with the noise of twenty-odd kids, the stillness of the forest calmed Seth. The woods seemed like a place where he could safely disappear for a while. He's wanted to go back ever since.

Now's his chance. But his one-zone transfer isn't enough to get him there. When the bus to Sooke arrives, he boards and spends half of what he's got left on the fare. The bus travels up the island highway, passing the waters of the Gorge Inlet on one side and the Galloping Goose bike trail on the other. The driver picks up speed until the turn-off into Langford with its big-box stores. When the malls and their sprawling parking lots finally end, the bus follows a winding, tree-lined road, passing hobby farms and the T'Sou-ke First Nation. After more than an hour, it arrives at the village centre with its plazas, grocery store, and coffee shops. The end of the line is coming soon, so Seth steps off the bus.

A zing of adrenaline shoots through him. He's a long way from home. No one knows where he is. For once, he feels free.

He catches sight of a clock: it's quarter to six. No wonder he's hungry! He's standing in front of a pizza-by-the-slice place, and the smell makes his mouth water. He rummages in his pocket and finds enough change for a slice.

At a table outside the restaurant, he downs half a slice of pepperoni pizza in thirty seconds flat. He should have gone into the grocery store instead; he could have stretched the money a lot farther. He tries to slow down his chewing and make it last.

At the next table, a couple of kids around his age are sharing a can of Coke and talking.

"My cousin said he'd drive us back to the rez."

"He kept us waiting for two hours last time! Let's just hitch."

Seth listens hard. When one of them glances at him and nods, he realizes he's been staring. He looks down at his paper plate.

The other boy turns back to his friend. They argue until the first boy gives in with a shrug. "Okay. Let's go."

Seth watches them head down to the shoulder of the road and walk west toward the edge of town. Once they turn to face oncoming traffic and stick their thumbs out, they get picked up within a few minutes. They're heading in the direction Seth wants to go.

He wishes he had more money and some gear — a sleeping bag, even a blanket. But the day has been warm and dry. He won't freeze tonight.

He waits ten minutes and then heads down to the spot where the two boys hitched a ride. He sticks out his thumb. Several cars speed past without slowing down. *What do I have to do to get a ride around here?*

He realizes he's scowling and slouching, which can't be helping his chances of getting picked up. He relaxes his face and straightens up. After a few more cars pass, a Chrysler sedan pulls over. He runs to the passenger side door and opens it.

A wave of lavender perfume hits him. A white-haired, elderly woman is holding the steering wheel at ten and two. She turns her head. "Did you miss the bus to Pacheedaht?"

Confused, Seth shakes his head.

"My mistake. I thought you were one of the boys from the First Nation by Port Renfrew. They have to bus nearly two hours each way!"

"That's rough," Seth says.

The lady sizes him up. "Where is it that you're going, then?"

"Me?" For a moment, Seth can't remember.

"I'm going as far as the Jordan," she says.

"That's great." Seth hopes that's far enough. He remembers to add, "I'm going to China Beach."

The old woman raises her white eyebrows. "Oh?"

"Yes, I, um," Seth says. "I missed my ride. My friends, they — they forgot I was coming."

She looks him over. "I hope they have your equipment."

Seth blushes. He hates lying to little old ladies. "I'm sharing a tent with my buddy."

"Hop in then."

Seth climbs in, sets his backpack on his lap, and pulls the heavy door shut behind him. As the lady pulls onto the road, the seat hardly bounces at all. The radio is playing something cheesy that the lady hums along to.

*She thought I was from a First Nation — at least when she saw me from a distance.* The hairs prickle on the back of his neck. During the search for his birth mom, he kept Googling "adopted from foster care." He learned that about half of the kids in care are Aboriginal. Authorities try to place them with Aboriginal families, but there aren't enough homes available. He doesn't know if he was one of those kids or not. He might never know. Best case scenario, he's got three years to wait. He sighs.

The lady glances at him. "Do you like camping?"

Seth usually sleeps in a tent in the backyard when he visits his dad because there's no extra room. He's not sure if that counts as camping. "I don't know," he says. "I've hardly ever done it."

"I don't blame you. Country living is rustic enough, what with splitting wood for the stove and chasing bears out of the yard. I don't like to give up my mattress on top of it."

Seth gulps. "Bears?"

The lady glances over and chuckles at Seth's expression. "Keep your food packed away and they won't bother you."

Seth nods. *So there's an upside to having no food.* He might starve, but at least he won't get mauled to death.

When the sign for the China Beach campground looms up, the lady turns left and pulls in. The campsites near the entrance are occupied, and a few kids are kicking a soccer ball on the drive.

"Are you sure your friends are here?" the lady asks.

Seth nods. "Definitely. Thank you for the ride!"

He slides out of the car and waves as the lady does a U-turn. He stands in the middle of the gravel road, hands in his jacket pockets. Spindly evergreens tower over him. The kids with the soccer ball rake him with their eyes. Seth wishes he'd made a better plan.

"Hello there!"

With a start, Seth glances over his shoulder. A man who looks like a Cub Scout leader is bearing down on him, holding a clipboard. Seth makes a break for the woods.

# CHAPTER 4

# Brooke: Escape

"Brooke?" Her mother's voice sounds just outside the bedroom door. "Are you all right?"

During dinner, Brooke looked at her plate and gave one-word answers to her parents' questions. She retreated to her room as soon as the meal was over. She should've known her mom would get suspicious. "Yeah, Mom, I'm fine."

Her mom turns the doorknob and peeks into Brooke's room. "Your dad and I are going grocery shopping. Do you need anything?"

*A home pregnancy test.* Brooke chokes back a nervous laugh. "No, I'm good."

A few minutes later, her parents' sedan backs out of the driveway. Brooke watches from the window. The golden light of early evening slants into the yard. Kelly-green maple leaves glow as they dangle from branches.

Her period is probably just late, but what if it's not? She needs time to absorb the shock. She needs time to think. She'll eventually have to make a decision.

Brooke flops onto her bed and stares in front of her. Her eyes fall on the pile of backpacking gear in her closet. The summer before, she saved up her money and bought everything she would need to hike the Juan de Fuca Marine Trail, a wilderness trek northwest of the city. She planned to backpack over the Labour Day weekend with Adam, her friend Erika, and Erika's boyfriend. She read the guidebook from cover to cover to prepare. But at the last minute, Brooke's mom vetoed the trip. She assumed Brooke and Adam would be sharing a tent. "I just can't condone it," she said. And by "it," she meant teenaged sex. *As if the trip was about that.*

Brooke still longs to do a multiday hike, one that would immerse her in nature. Daytrips just aren't the same: everyone says so. There's something primal and healing and *real* about leaving behind electricity, plumbing, and the digital world — not just for a few hours, but for days.

She sits bolt upright. *That's it!* She'll head out to the trail tonight. *It's the perfect escape.*

She manages to fit the tent inside her pack along with freeze-dried bags of lasagna, chicken, and chili. She tucks in her hiking clothes. The outer pockets of the pack are already filled with supplies like matches, insect repellent, and a water purification kit. Next, she has to tie the sleeping bag to the top of the pack. She cinches the straps up tight. *Damn.* She forgot the foamie. She loosens the straps and yanks the sleeping bag out.

She has to be out the door before her parents get home. Her mom's been known to park the car right behind Brooke's, trapping it in the driveway. Her mom has never tried to stop Deanna from doing anything. Deanna is the responsible daughter who makes good choices. Brooke scrunches her nose. She needs to get away from her mother. Scratch that. Away from everyone.

Her phone rings, and she checks the call display. *Adam.* She lets the voice mail pick up as she keeps packing. Then she plays back the message.

"Hey Brooke, what's up? I'm just leaving the gym. I'll stop by your place in case you're home. Maybe we can go grab a bite to eat."

*Shit.* Now she has only ten minutes. Brooke deletes the message. She throws twine, sleeping bag, foamie, rope, hiking boots, and water bottle into a gym bag. She'll repack at the trailhead.

She's on the road by just after seven o'clock. On the drive out of town, Brooke pictures the trail in her mind. It stretches for forty-seven kilometres along the west coast of Vancouver Island. The photos show sweeping beaches and curling surf, an endless coastline of trees and rocks, streams that cascade off cliff tops to the sand. She'll hike in, leave civilization behind, and listen to the waves crash. She'll have time to herself — time to think. *It'll be heaven.*

In Sooke, she stops at a grocery store and stocks up on a few items: oranges, plums, trail mix, frozen burritos, veggie bacon, and toilet paper. Chocolate, too. Her phone rings as she's shopping, but she ignores it. A few seconds later, a text message arrives with a buzz. She taps the screen and reads the message.

W r u? R u ok?

She chews her lower lip. What to say? Adam won't understand why she's running from him.

At the check-out counter, she withdraws forty dollars of extra cash for the camp fees. Good thing she was able to save most of what she made last summer.

On a bench outside the store, she pulls out her phone. While she still has a signal, she needs to reply to Adam.

Her phone buzzes again. It's her dad this time.

Adam came by looking for you. You with Erika?

She didn't even think of inviting Erika. The two of them are buddies, but they aren't BFFs. Maybe some girls share the details of their cycles, but Brooke can't imagine texting Erika, *"OMG my . is l8!"*

She types back.

On my own. Hiking JdF. But I'LL B FINE!

Her dad will have to find a way to break the news to her mom. After two decades, he's pretty good at it.

She types another message.

Adam, I'm ok. Just need 2 b alone 4 a bit.

She hesitates. She knows what he wants to hear. Does it matter if she's feeling it? Probably not.

Love u.

Brooke shuts off her phone. She's bought herself some time. Back on the open road, her shoulders drop. The sun is sinking, and she still has miles to go.

# CHAPTER 5

# Seth: Crow

Seth shivers in the early morning cold. His teeth are chattering. The night before, he hiked until dark, and then it was hard to find anywhere to sleep that was remotely dry, let alone cozy. The best he could do was wedge himself in between a fallen log and a boulder. He barely slept. The woods rustled with life: crawling insects, snapping twigs, and snuffling noses. Cold and freaked out, he shivered all night. He must have dozed because he woke up at first light, frozen stiff.

His hands and nose are still numb. If only he had a toque. Hunger pangs claw the lining of his stomach. The inside of his mouth is parched. He finds the trail and walks just because he's too cold to stand still.

A crow lands on the path in front of him. It tilts its head and stares at him. Its body seems long, and its wings swoop into points behind it like the stern of a boat. The jet-black feathers gleam with a blue sheen. It opens its beak. Instead of a caw, it makes a rattling sound. It doesn't sound much like the crows at home. *Could it be a raven?* Seth doesn't really know how to tell them apart.

The bird jumps up on spring-loaded legs and flaps its wings. In a few strokes, it lands high in a tree that's several metres into the forest, off the trail. It pauses there, resting on a branch. Is it waiting for Seth?

*Don't be stupid. One night in the woods and you think the animals are sending you signals?*

Seth continues along the trail. Head down, he passes the tree where the crow is perched and keeps on going. Before he can travel out of earshot, the bird cries again. Not the rattling sound this time, but a series of caws. It sounds like an alarm. It's as if the crow is warning him not to travel in that direction.

He pivots and dodges until he catches sight of the bird halfway up a Douglas fir tree. He takes a deep breath that makes his shoulders rise and fall. Something tells him to follow the crow. *Animals must know where to find fresh water, right?* Maybe he's losing his mind, but then again, it's not like he has a better plan. Keeping his eyes on the crow, he moves into the bush toward it.

Before long, he whacks his shin on a fallen log. "Ow!" Seth hops on his good leg, clutching his shin. *That's what you get for watching a stupid bird instead of watching where you're going!* Once the pain fades, he reaches under his pant leg and feels the swelling pushing up on his shin. From a treetop several metres away comes a chuckling sound. At least, it sure sounds like chuckling.

Seth sits down on the log that slammed his shin. Getting laughed at for hurting himself — he's been *there* before. A few months ago, his mom had the brilliant idea that her a-hole boyfriend Bert should take Seth fishing. *Male bonding,* she called it. Bert was supposed to teach him how to club a fish to death in the bottom of a boat. By accident, Seth clubbed his own foot. Rhymes-with-hurt thought that was hilarious. It was so painful that Seth limped for weeks.

He slumps forward and drops his forehead into the heels of his hands. "Focus, man." The sound of his own voice startles him. It feels like days since he last spoke or heard another person talk. "You've got to hold it together."

But it's hard to stop the memories. He hasn't told his mom about Bert's cruel ways, just like he never told on Keith back in foster care. When he was little, all he did was silently hope that his birth mom would show up to take him home. Even if he and Keith shared a dad, his mom belonged to Seth alone.

His birth mom never came. Instead, when he was seven, the Migliozzis adopted him. Things got better for a while. Patches was just a puppy back then, and Seth took to him right away. His dad taught him how to take care of the dog, and they walked him together every day. Strangers couldn't tell he was adopted. At his new school, his teacher read out his last name and said, "You're Italian! So am I." His dad had black hair, brown eyes, and what his mom called "olive skin," which turned darker than Seth's in the summer. When he and his dad were together, people would look back and forth from one to the other and smile, like they could see the family resemblance. It felt good to belong.

As for his mom, not being able to have a child had made her unhappy. Adopting Seth was supposed to fix everything, but it seemed like nothing he or his dad did was ever enough. When Seth's dad started driving a long-haul truck and spending nights away from home, his mom blamed Seth. Every time he did something wrong, it was the same: "Look at the mess you made with that spaghetti sauce! No wonder your dad can't stand to be at home anymore." It got worse and worse until his parents finally split about a year ago. A few months after that, Bert came along. Now, on bad days, Seth feels like he's right back where he was before the adoption.

He's gathering his strength to keep going when he hears the crow's voice again. He turns his head, and it's there — on the far end of the log he's sitting on. One beady black eye takes him in. Seth fights an urge to throw something at it. The bird shifts from one foot to the other. With a click of its vocal chords, it springs up and flies into the forest. This time, it lands on a nearer tree. It looks back at Seth. "Grr-k-k-k." The rattling call carries a reedy tune.

"What do you want?" Seth grumbles. He doesn't get an answer. But he hauls himself to his feet and follows the bird anyway.

# CHAPTER 6

# Brooke: Bear

Brooke stretches her arms over her head and bumps the wall of the nylon tent. She rolls her neck from side to side. It has definitely developed a kink overnight, and the tip of her nose has gone numb with cold. Otherwise, she feels pretty good.

Then reality floods back. Her period is late. She slides her hand inside her underwear to check for blood, but her fingertip comes back clean. Her body feels tight, like a water balloon filled to the bursting point. When she rolls onto her side, she squishes her breast, and the quick stab of pain makes her gasp.

Tears well up. The stress of school, the pressure of job-hunting, the constant nagging from her mom. Even Adam's soft pleas and promises. And now this . . . this potential disaster. It's all too much.

Adam will still be asleep — unless he's too upset by her vanishing act. Like her mom must be. Guilt claws at her chest. But then a wave of anger flushes it out. She's done with being pressured by the two of them.

She wriggles into her shirt and hiking pants. She unzips

the door to her tent and slides her feet into her boots. The air smells pine-scented and earthy. The sun hasn't crested the treetops yet. It has to be around seven o'clock.

It isn't out of the question that Adam — or even her dad — will show up at the campground looking for her. It's time to hit the trail. No hot breakfast today. She'll munch on an energy bar when she gets hungry.

After a trip to the outhouse, she rolls up her sleeping bag and foamie and yanks the poles from her tent. Within minutes, she's repacked everything. She laces her hiking boots up tight. She loops both arms through the straps of the backpack and hauls it in front of her like a sack of rice until she reaches the water tap. She drops the pack, fills her plastic water bottle, and tucks it into an outer pocket.

Beside the tap, a wooden placard shows the route. She takes a small paper copy of the trail map from a dispenser. The next camping spot is a wilderness site nine kilometres away. She does a double-take at its name.

Bear Beach.

A laminated plastic sign has been stuck to the board with a thumbtack: WARNING — BEAR IN AREA.

Brooke's stomach flip-flops. The guidebook mentioned that this trail runs through bear country. But it's one thing to read about bears — it's another thing to face them. Alone. The sign reminds her how to behave:

*Never surprise a bear. Make warning noises.*

She forgot to bring a bear bell. Will she have to shout the whole time?

*If you see a bear, do not approach it. Talk softly and back away slowly. If attacked by a black bear, do not play dead. Attempt to escape.*

Bears aren't all there is to worry about, either.

*If you see a cougar, do not attempt to run away. Raise your arms, speak loudly and firmly, and wave a stick. Try to appear larger than you are.*

She shudders. This trail snakes all the way to Port Renfrew. It zig-zags up hills and down gullies. It spans hundred-foot-high suspension bridges. It crosses beaches accessible only at low tide. If something goes wrong, she could be in serious trouble. Hiking alone is risky. Even experienced backpackers rarely take solo trips. Her mom's question rings in her ears: *What are you, suicidal?*

She breathes in and out slowly. Four days of steady walking will get her from one end to the other. It will be four days of freedom. Four days of escape — from her mother, from the job hunt, from Adam. From the worrying dates on the calendar.

*I'm doing this.*

She presses hard to fill in the registration form with a pen that's running out of ink. Into the envelope, she tucks the forty dollars she withdrew at the grocery store. She rips off the receipt and drops the envelope into the lock box.

Now to figure out some kind of noisemaker so that animals hear her coming. She bends down and fishes her cooking pots out of her pack. With her spare piece of twine, she rigs them up to rattle and bang against each other with every step she takes. She hoists her pack onto a boulder, turns around, bends her knees, and backs into it. She slips her arms through the shoulder straps, cinches the belt, and fastens the chest strap. With a heave, she stands up and takes her first steps down the trail.

A path about four feet wide cuts through the second-growth

forest. The evergreens — Douglas firs along with a few cedars — grow so thick and tall that they block all but a glimpse of sky. Not much sunlight filters down to the forest floor. Roots criss-cross the path, so she has to keep her head down and watch her step. She just puts one foot in front of the other. The pack weighs on her shoulders, but the ground springs back underfoot. *Ca-thunk, clatter-ump. Ca-thunk, clatter-ump.* The melody of the pot and pan soothe her.

Underneath the clanging sounds, a stream gushes. She bounces her way over the suspension bridge high above Pete Wolf Creek. Within an hour, she's descending a steep hill to Mystic Beach. A felled tree serves as a staircase. One side is sawed flat and cross-hatched to make footholds. She inches her way down the log, holding her arms out for balance. After a few more twists and turns in the path, the beach opens up.

Grey-brown sand stretches out flat before her. The surf rolls in. She picks her way over the drift logs, unbuckles her pack, and lets it drop. She hears a waterfall behind her and turns. Her eyes trace the cascade up a cliff the height of a three-storey building. On the cliff top stands a bear. It shifts its weight and tosses its head.

At first, only her knees shake. Soon she's quivering all over. She shrugs into her pack and hurries toward the opposite end of the beach before she remembers. *I'm supposed to "back away slowly!" Hard to do when you're terrified.* She hopes she hasn't provoked the bear. At least there's a cliff between them.

She's forced to slow down when the sand tapers into a bed of wet stones. They're bound to be slick. A few steps further on, the wet patch expands into a creek, shallow but wide. She picks her way from one stone to the next, bearing down on the centre of her foot. Falling onto rocks with a thirty-pound pack on her back would really hurt. But she makes it across without slipping.

On the far side of the creek, she glances back at the cliff. The bear has disappeared. Brooke trembles as she digs an energy bar out of a side pocket in her pack. She leans against a log and gobbles it down. After she's finished eating, she takes deep breaths to calm herself. *He's more scared of me than I am of him.* As long as her noise-maker does its work, she'll be fine.

An orange buoy marks the spot to re-enter the trail. She scales the bank, pulsing with confidence. *Bear or no bear, I can do this!*

## CHAPTER 7

# Seth: Hot spring

The crow has led Seth to the edge of a cliff that plunges to a narrow inlet. A tree with half its roots exposed leans out over the water, nearly horizontal. On its trunk sits the crow, fixing Seth with its black gaze. Does it want him follow it *there,* too? The water churns about twelve feet below.

The cliff is steep, but it's made of earth, not rock, which means it has footholds — knobs, bushes, and patches of wild grass. Seth scans the cliff below him and extends his toe toward a foothold. Just as he's about to slide his weight down, he catches a whiff of something. *Rotten egg!* The surprise throws him off, and he slides on his butt, grasping at anything he can. A stick breaks off in his hand, and a clump of grass tears out of the ground. He clutches a fistful of dirt as he bumps along, gaining momentum.

He sails past the crow and freefalls for twelve feet before splashing into the sea. It's so cold that he shouts. His backpack, clothes, and shoes absorb water and drag on him. His teeth chatter. His fingers grow numb and stiff like they're encased in ice. He sputters and dogpaddles to the side of the channel. He finds only steep-sided, seaweed-covered rocks that he can't pull himself up on. *This is what I get for trusting a crow.* He treads water, breathing heavily.

The rotten-egg smell again! And a waft of steam. A trickle of water drains steadily into the channel. Seth can't quite see where it's coming from. He paddles toward it. A narrow stream trickles down the cliff into the ocean. He gets close enough to feel the water on his shoulders — and it's warm, he's pretty sure it's warm, unless his numb skin is tricking him. His head aches with cold, so he dogpaddles under the stream and lets it splash his head. *Dude, that's definitely heat.* It feels so good that he doesn't mind the stink.

But he's tiring fast. Just beyond the stream, a shelf about two inches wide sticks out from the rock face. He grasps it with both hands and pulls himself up. Another shelf juts out within reach, so he clasps it with his right hand and draws his left foot up to the first shelf. His waterlogged clothes weigh him down. His biceps quiver with the strain of hauling himself out of the water. The rock finally levels out to a flat surface that's big enough to lie on. He shimmies up until he's fully free of the ocean. He lies flat on his stomach, panting, heart racing. He could have drowned. He could have easily drowned.

After he catches his breath, he pulls himself up to sit cross-legged. He whiffs rotten egg again. A few feet ahead of him, steaming water flows across the rock shelf and falls into the ocean. Upstream, a hole gapes in the rock face. It looks like the mouth of a cave. He crawls toward it and looks in. He was right! It's a dome-shaped cave. The roof arches high over a pool of water. He strips off his wet things and drops them in a pile outside the entrance to the cave. Naked, he ducks inside.

He sinks in the water up to his neck, letting its warmth soak into his skin and heat up his cold, aching bones.

He floats across the pool to where the water is gushing from the wall of the cave. He sets his hand into the stream, and it's *hot*. It pours over his hand. It's hard to believe water can get this hot just from being inside the earth. It seems magical, but it's real. It's even crazier to think that the crow might have guided him here. *But maybe it did.* He sinks back down to his neck.

When the sun breaks through the clouds, he climbs out and scoops up his clothes. They're cold and wet and he can't stand to put them on. He spreads everything on a slope of black rock: his backpack, shirt, pants, jacket, underwear, shoes, and socks. He surveys them.

The day after the Migliozzis adopted him, they bought him a whole wardrobe. He didn't mind the new clothes, but, without asking him, his mom got rid of his old ones, including his favourite t-shirt and his comfy, broken-in jeans. She also insisted on a haircut, even though he liked his shaggy style. *She never accepted me for who I was. She tried to change me into the perfect son so that she could have the perfect family. And when it didn't work out, it was all my fault. As usual.*

A gust of wind off the ocean makes him shiver. It flips over one sleeve of his shirt. He might lose his clothes and his backpack if he doesn't do something. He'll need rocks about the size of grapefruit to tack everything down.

As he searches for rocks, the sun creeps higher in the sky, and its rays gather strength. When he has gathered enough stones, he pins down his backpack and his clothes and sits back on his heels. A thread of steam twists up from the cuff of his pant leg. Seth yelps. *It's going to work!* A faint glow fills his chest. He's figured something out on his own, and for once his mom isn't here to tell him how badly he's screwed it up.

He smacks his lips, which feel gummy. He can't remember when he last had a drink. He needs to find fresh water, soon. Creeks empty into the ocean, so all he has to do is sweep the coast until he finds one. *Simple.*

He steps into his Jockeys, his flesh shrinking from the clammy cotton and wet elastic as he drags them up his legs. *Ick.* His waterlogged running shoes squelch and pull at the skin on the tops of his feet. He grimaces. *It sucks that everything got soaked. But it was worth it to find that hot spring.* With a pool to warm up in, he won't freeze to death out here.

Climbing back up to the top of the cliff is pretty easy. He turns left. He has to bushwhack, and soon he's sorry he didn't pull on the rest of his wet clothes. He's getting scratched all over. Welts swell up on his arms and legs, and they really sting.

He treks on, losing track of the distance, but always keeping the ocean on his left. There has to be fresh water *somewhere* along this coast. He follows the twists and turns of the headland until, finally, he hears a creek. It's all the way down at sea level, flowing at the bottom of a deep gulley lined with fern.

He bends his knees and keeps the soles of his shoes in contact with the earth as he shuffles downhill. The fast-flowing water looks clear and delicious. He kicks off his shoes and walks right into it. The cold water shocks his calves as he bends to scoop handfuls to his mouth. It tastes sweet. As it glides down his throat, it's like being able to breathe again.

He drinks until he starts to feel sick to his stomach. A nearby rock stretches flat and smooth like a stool, and he collapses to sit on it, head in his hands. The creek thunders on, blocking out all other sound. Seth waits until the water has settled in his stomach. He can't remember when he last peed. But before too long, a twinge in his bladder makes him stagger to his feet. He's so tired and foggy-headed that he pees on the spot.

"Hey!" It's a female voice, shouting.

# CHAPTER 8

# Brooke: Mud

"Hey!" Brooke yells again.

A young, bare-chested guy behind the bushes on the opposite bank flicks his head. He shakes his heavy brown hair out of his eyes.

"What are you peeing in the stream for? I was filling up my water bottle. You've got the whole forest to use!"

But Brooke is yelling into the wind. The guy has vanished. She crosses the bridge and bushwhacks her way to where he was standing. There's no trace of him. Was she seeing things?

She takes a few more steps upstream before filling her bottle, to be on the safe side. She unzips the black case that holds the water filtration pump. The lengths of rubber hose and the disassembled parts confuse her. She hasn't looked at the kit since last year, when she spent an hour putting it together and trying to pump water from the bathtub. She'll figure it out later. *The tablets will have to do this time.*

She pops one in, shakes the bottle, and settles in to wait

while the water purifies. As she nibbles on trail mix, the gushing of the stream lulls her.

The first sip of treated water makes her choke. It tastes like sulphur mixed with iron, and she spits it out. Untreated stream water would probably taste fresh and delicious. But until she masters the water pump, she's stuck with the foul-tasting stuff. It's too bad, because all this hiking makes her really thirsty.

She forces down a few more mouthfuls and hoists on the pack. After the break, it takes time for her legs to get into a rhythm again. Just when she's got her momentum back, she rounds a bend and halts.

In front of her lies a mud puddle. Make that, a mud *pond*. The trail is completely flooded. She spread-eagles her legs, one foot on either side of the pond, and inches forward like a water spider. But the mud patch widens. Her legs are straddled so far that she's stuck. She seizes a branch so she can haul herself to one side of the swamp. She gives it some weight to test it, but when she pushes off with the opposite foot and pulls on the branch, it gives way and she falls hard into the mucky puddle.

The mud smears her legs, her pants, her arms, and her pack. She groans. Except for a pair of shorts, she doesn't have a change of clothes. *This is too hard!* Seeing a bear scared her senseless, but at least it gave her an adrenaline rush. Hiking in mud is a pure slog. If she turns around now, she could be back at the car in a few hours.

*And what would I tell Mom and Dad? "I couldn't handle it. Guess I'm too much of a wimp for Adventure Studies, after all. Nursing, here I come." No way!*

Besides, the worst has happened. There's no point trying to stay clean anymore, so she just plods down the middle of the puddle, shin-deep, until her boots and calves are slathered in mud. Eventually, the trail dries up again.

By early afternoon, Brooke's legs feel like cement. Every time she raises her head to take in the scenery, she's at the mercy of roots, mud slicks, and fallen logs. She has to keep her eyes on the ground. Beside the trail, orange metal plates nailed to low brown posts mark the kilometres. She could swear it has been an hour since she saw the last marker, for kilometre five. Most likely, she passed kilometre six without noticing it.

On the other hand, she hasn't met any other hikers for a couple of hours. Could she have wandered off the path? Her thighs burn and her swollen feet press the seams of her hiking boots. Blisters have risen on both heels. What she really needs to do is stop for the day and soak her feet in sea water.

She catches a flash of orange up ahead. *Phew. I'm not lost.* The marker will read *7 km*, she's sure. There's no way she's gone only one kilometre in the past hour. She draws level with the post.

*6 km.*

She groans out loud but restrains herself. *Don't fall apart. You can do this. Just three more kilometres to go.*

Around the next bend, she finds yet another steep, muddy incline. It looks like a slide made of mud. This time, she cries out loud, "Not again!" Then she studies the hill more closely. Sawed-up rounds of tree trunk dot the hillside like a rough staircase. On the reddish-brown wood, rings radiate from the centre, one for every year of the tree's life. She gives thanks to the trees and to whoever put the wood there. She's mustering her strength to climb the hill when she hears voices behind her.

"Two-thirds of the way there!"

She half-turns. A young couple bounds down the trail, lively as colts. They stop when they reach her. The girl adjusts her bandana and says, "Hi there."

The guy takes a sip of water from his camel pack. "Took a tumble, huh?" He sounds pleased, as if her fall confirms his own skill.

Brooke glances at her feet. Her boots look like chocolate fondue gone wrong. She wishes she didn't feel the need to defend herself. "Tough stretch of trail."

The fresh-faced boy glances at his girlfriend, then turns back to Brooke. "You come from China Beach today?"

She nods.

"How long you been on the trail?"

It seems like an innocent question. "Four hours."

"Woot!" He high-fives his girlfriend. "We started at China two and a half hours ago."

Brooke grits her teeth. *Jerk.*

The girl grins and shrugs her shoulders. "He's a slave-driver."

Her limbs are slender, golden-brown, and spotless. They show no signs of suffering, or even effort.

As the mud on Brooke's legs dries and cakes, it pulls on her skin and itches. "Do you know if the trail levels out between here and Bear Beach?"

"Not really," the boy says.

The girl smiles apologetically. "Hang in there." The pair scales the hill and disappears before Brooke finds the energy to start the climb.

# CHAPTER 9

# Seth: Hunger

The return trip to the hot spring seems to take half the time. After the shouting girl left, Seth came out of hiding to drink his fill from the stream. Like a wilted plant that gets watered, he has straightened up. He feels energized.

He checks the clothes he left pegged under the rocks. *As dry as they're ever going to be.* He unlaces his sneakers, the shoestrings crusty and stiff to the touch. He wriggles into the damp pants that seem to have shrunk and tightened up with the salt water. He shrugs into his shirt and jacket. He pokes his toe into the neck of his sock to widen it before he pulls it on. He shoves his feet back into his shoes and ties them up. He slings his damp knapsack over his shoulders. *Falling into the ocean fully clothed? Yeah. Not such a smart idea.*

But the saltwater smell that clings to his clothes is fresher than the sulphur smell, and as he starts to move, the fabric warms up and molds to his body a little better. Pretty soon he doesn't notice the feel of the clothes against his skin. There's too much else to focus on.

Like food.

He searches the cliff-side for something edible. Moss-green anemones cluster into the deep corners of a crevice. They sit like sea flowers underwater. Above green bases and stems, pink tendrils open like petals and wave ever so slightly. They look like strands of grapefruit, like the pulp under the inner skin, the pieces that get caught between your teeth. Seth's mouth waters — *the juice would taste so good!*

He crouches down. He stretches one hand into the water and touches the outermost tendril of an anemone with his finger. The flower folds up tight like a green bud.

Seth yanks his hand back. He didn't know it was alive! Not in that way, not like an animal. He thought it was a plant.

His stomach growls, like it too has a life of its own. He can't rip that animal-flower off the side of the rock *now* — can he? It does look awfully defenceless. But then . . . if it were good to eat, why would it still be sitting there, not picked off by a shore bird?

Beyond the sea-flower, deeper into the water, floats a bed of kelp. An olive-green bulb acts like a buoy, keeping the plant afloat on the surface. And this time, he *knows* it's a plant. It's a type of seaweed. He's pretty sure, anyway, that it's not going to duck and bob of its own power when he touches it.

He inches around to a different rock, thankful for the grip on the rubber soles of his running shoes. He reaches into the water and grabs hold of a long, greenish-brown strand of sea-weed. It's like a giant spinach lasagna noodle floating on the water. He grasps a slippery edge and yanks. He pulls the leaf toward him, hand over hand. He wants to get that crispy olive-green bulb. He could sink his teeth into it like an *apple*. It won't come to him, though. There's too much resistance, and the leaf keeps snapping back.

So he turns the leaf. It's about six feet long and rectangular, shaped like a ribbon, or a scarf. He tears it across. It doesn't rip cleanly, it's too sinewy, but bit by bit the leaf separates and he drags it back up to the cliff top.

He sits cross-legged on the rock next to his clothes. He holds up the kelp, and the ocean smell makes him wrinkle his nose. But it's just a salty vegetable. He likes to salt his peas, doesn't he? He opens his mouth and tears at the kelp with his teeth. Salt tickles his tongue. The kelp tastes like the ocean smells.

He manages to tear off a piece with his teeth. The leaf is tough and rubbery. He chews and chews, but it doesn't seem to break down.

After several minutes of gnawing, he finally swallows, hoping he won't choke. The fibre works its way down his esophagus as he bites off a new piece and chews it. His jaw is getting sore. Will kelp do anything to satisfy his hunger? *Fat chance. It's too much like trying to fill up on celery.* He tried that once when his mom blew the grocery money on a new dress, and celery was the only thing left to eat. When his dad got home from his road trip, he ignored the new dress, but he sure noticed the empty fridge. He reamed out his mom about "starving the boy" and then took Seth to McDonald's.

His mouth waters at the memory of hamburger. He's going to have to get some protein soon. Depending on how long he stays out here — how long he survives — he may have to start living off the sea. Bert showed him how to harvest mussels — all he needs is a knife. *That's one thing the bastard was good for.* Problem is, in a red tide, shellfish can kill you. "And not all red tides are red," Bert had said, laughing. "I call it Mussel Roulette. Want to play?" For now, Seth has got to find a campground. *Backpackers will have food.*

Seth weaves his way through the bush, heading for the main trail where travelling will be easier and quicker. As he approaches a break in the forest that signals the path, the sound of voices makes him freeze. He can just glimpse people through the trees.

A male voice booms, "Hello there! Park ranger. Can I see your permits, please?" With a flash of blue and red, backpacks are lowered and pockets are unzipped. The backpackers murmur a question.

"That's right," the ranger says. "Ten dollars per person per night."

Seth's heart speeds up. *The trail is patrolled?* He can't pay the fees. Even if he says he's on a day hike, the ranger's bound to get suspicious. With his street shoes and his lack of gear, he's not very convincing as a hiker. The ranger might ask how he got out here and why he's hiking alone. If he doesn't buy Seth's answers, he could report him as a runaway. Seth's not going to let that happen. From now on, he'll stick to the bush, or the beach.

Before anyone sees him, he retreats back to the shoreline. He scrambles down a cliff and picks his way along a rocky stretch of coast. When the beach ends in another cliff, he climbs up and clings to the side of it. His fingers reach for handholds and the toes of his sneakers fumble for footholds. As he moves sideways across the vertical rock face, he tries not to think about falling. The waves bob and nip at his feet. The next campsite is on a beach, so he'll get there eventually. He just hopes he makes it before his hands cramp up.

# CHAPTER 10

# Brooke: Real Time

As Brooke crests the final hill before Bear Beach, a half-moon of white sand reveals itself. Arbutus trees, with their twisting auburn trunks and limbs, line the path below. She descends on shaking legs, passing kilometre nine just before she reaches the shore.

She told herself she was coming out here to think, but she hasn't been able to let her mind drift. She has to concentrate, or she'll lose her way, trip on a root, or run out of water. Every step of the way, she has to be on guard.

The way she wasn't that night with Adam.

She drops her pack on the beach and flops onto her back in a starfish shape. The ebb and flow of the surf lull her. Just before she drifts to sleep, she shakes herself awake and stands up. She still needs to search out a tenting spot. She hoists on her pack, bending almost double with the weight. At first glance, the beach is deserted, but as she trudges along, individual campsites come into view under the trees, screened from the beach by snowberry and salal bushes. Tents fill most of the cubbyholes, but eventually she finds a spot to claim as her own. The dirt floor is lined with pine needles. She sets to work fitting poles into sleeves, and soon her tent arches into a taut green dome. She takes a deep breath. *Home sweet home.*

She unlaces her boots, steps out of them, and peels off her socks. At the ankle, a ring of dirt gives way to feet that look surprisingly clean. She strips off her pants and pulls on a pair of clean walking shorts. She digs out her sandals and a towel, along with her water filter and bottle, and ducks through the screen of bushes to the beach.

The map showed a creek, so Brooke heads north. Or is it west? Feeling weightless without the pack, she floats along. Rivulets branch through the sand, draining toward the ocean. She turns and traces them inland until they swell into a stream a foot deep.

The girl in the bandana squats on the bank, a filtration pump on her lap. "Hey."

Brooke sinks down beside her. "Hey." She's too exhausted to be shy. "Can I see how you do that?" The girl's water pump looks similar to her own.

"Sure."

The girl holds it up and twists it so Brooke can see how the parts fit together. She grips it in one hand and pumps with the other, sucking water up from the river to gush into a clear plastic bottle. Each stroke produces a spurt so small that filling up the bottle will take several minutes.

Brooke picks up her own water filter and attaches hoses, valves, and the handle's collar. She treats it like Lego. If the pieces won't fit together, she gives up and tries another position. When they cinch up snug with a click, she knows — at least, she hopes — she's got it right.

"Everything sure takes time on the trail, huh?" Glancing at the other girl's equipment, Brooke adjusts the float and drops the hose into the creek. It gasps and sucks at first, but soon, at every stroke, water squirts into the bottle.

The girl nods. "This is 'real time.' No motors to speed things up."

Brooke loses count of how many times she presses the handle. Pumping water as the creek flows past is like falling into a trance — except for the ache in her arm.

Taking a break, she tugs off her sandals and dips her hot, swollen feet into the stream. It feels deliciously cold. She extends her legs and rinses some of the mud from her calves.

The other girl has finished pumping. She screws the lid onto her bottle and gets up to leave. "There's a waterfall at the far end of the beach," she says. "Great place to shower when things quiet down."

Standing naked at the foot of a cliff while cold water pelts her: the image makes Brooke's toes curl in anticipation. "Sounds fantastic."

The girl walks away, and Brooke calls out. "Hey!"

She looks back over her shoulder. "Yeah?"

"Thanks for your help with the filter."

The girl smiles. "You're totally welcome. Enjoy!"

With a full bottle of purified water, Brooke lopes back to her campsite. She unzips her tent, reaches into her food bag and closes her hand around a squishy, oblong shape. *A burrito. Thank god. That means I don't have to cook.*

She sits down cross-legged, tears off the plastic wrapper, and eats the burrito cold. The mushy beans and soggy wrap taste marvellous thanks to the main ingredient: salt. She crumples the empty wrapper in her hand. No dishes to wash, either. Her belly full, she crawls into her tent and stretches out.

Backpacking is a lot of work: she's either walking or meeting her basic needs. All the motion keeps her occupied and makes her too tired to think. It's a relief to be completely in the moment. But is she just avoiding the problem? Her hand slides to her belly. After all, she came out here to reflect on what's happened and decide what to do. Maybe now's the time to lie still and consider her options.

*Wrong.* She still has to cache her food. According to her guidebook, animals can smell it from a long way off. Not only bears and cougars, but rats and raccoons will claw their way into her tent if they're hungry enough. They might also mistake anything fragrant for something edible: shampoo, toothpaste, sunscreen, garbage. She stuffs everything smelly into a red drawstring sac and sets off up the beach.

# CHAPTER 11

# seth: food

From his perch on a cliff above Bear Beach, Seth surveys the tents pitched on the sand below. Just beyond the east end of the beach, over a bluff and out of sight, lies a tiny cove where he plans to sleep tonight under a rocky overhang. But before he can sleep, he needs to eat. Through the thick tangle of trees, he can just make out a brown wooden booth. It's tucked into the bush about twenty feet up from the beach. A guy with a shaved head emerges, and the door bangs shut behind him. *Must be an outhouse.* The guy disappears under the lip of the cliff.

Another brown structure stands near the outhouse: it's square and seems to be made of metal. It looks sort of like a mail delivery box with multiple cubby holes.

As he watches, a girl in a windbreaker and shorts appears through the bushes carrying a red fabric sac. Her dark brown ponytail swings as she approaches the metal box. She hesitates in front of it like she's not sure what to do. After a while, she reaches a hand in front of her, palm up, fingers pointing to the sky. Pushing up, her fingers disappear as if into a pocket. She lifts up a door and peers into whatever lies behind it. She lets the door drop with a clang. She tries another door and lets it drop, too. And another and another. Finally, she holds one of the doors open and stuffs in the bag. The door falls shut.

She turns back toward the beach, takes a few steps, and then halts. She spins around and, for a second, seems to be looking right at him. Seth scooches back, belly down, sending dirt and pebbles tumbling down the side of the hill below. He holds his breath. The moment passes, and she retraces her steps to the locker. She lifts up the handle, pulls out the red bag, yanks open the drawstring neck, and roots around inside it. She lifts her hand to her mouth, back and forth, her jaw moving.

*Yes! It's food. Practically all of those cubby holes must be full of it.* Seth's mouth waters as if he's the one eating handfuls of whatever it is. He tries to send the girl a telepathic message. *Leave some for me.*

Once she replaces the bag and leaves, it's really hard to wait. *Maybe the campers are done with the storage bins for the night.* But there's still a bit of light. If he's going to take food, he'd better do it after dark.

He tries to channel his inner cat burglar. He needs to be *patient* and *silent.* It'll be like tip-toeing to the kitchen for a midnight snack on one of the nights when, as a little kid, he was told to go to bed without any supper. That usually happened after fights with Keith. He had to pass his foster parents' bedroom. There was always a chance that his empty belly would choose that exact moment to let out one of its piercing wails. If it did, and his foster parents heard, there'd be worse punishment to follow.

Getting caught tonight would be awful, too. No doubt the backpackers would beat him up for stealing. Even if they felt sorry for him and let him go, it would be really embarrassing. He'll take only the smallest amount he can from each bin. *Maybe they won't even notice what's missing.*

When dusk thickens into night, he inches down the cliff. He picks his way to the food cache and lifts up the lid of a cubby hole. He snatches a white plastic bag. Before he can sample its contents, a beam of light bounces up and down as someone approaches from the beach. *Shit. So much for skimming food from a bunch of bins.* Seth quietly shuts the bin door, stuffs the plastic bag into his coat pocket, and walks on. He passes the person on the narrow trail.

"Hey." It's a deep male voice. "How's it going? No flashlight, huh?"

Seth keeps his head down. "Nope. I'm really roughing it."

The dude chuckles. "Right on. Have a good one, buddy."

Seth exhales. He's just been mistaken for a regular camper. The thought makes him smile.

On the beach, he stuffs handfuls of trail mix into his mouth. Sweet and salty flavours burst onto his tongue: peanuts, raisins, coconut, and chocolate chips. When the bag is empty, he turns it inside out and licks the corners. It sure feels good to have something in his stomach. Even though he could eat a lot more, his energy is flagging. It's time for bed. The open sky over the beach sheds a little bit of light, and the moon is rising over the treetops. All he has to do is walk the length of the beach, climb around the bluff, and he'll be safe in his private cove.

# CHAPTER 12

# Brooke: Relief

In the morning, a synthetic smell wafts from the nylon walls of her tent as they warm up in the sun. Brooke reaches overhead to unzip the door so that cool salt air blows in. As she shifts in her sleeping bag, pain drills into her lower back. It's no surprise that she's sore after six hours of hiking with a thirty pound pack yesterday. But she's bloated, too. She drags herself out of the tent, feeling dizzy. So much for trekking to the outhouse. She checks for other campers, then squats to pee in the bushes behind her tent.

Red smudges are showing in her underwear. Relief pours over her. The worry of being pregnant drops from her shoulders like a shucked-off backpack. The sudden lightness makes her want to shriek with joy.

But she didn't bring any tampons. *Idiot!*

She rummages in her pack for her Swiss army knife and her towel. By mistake, she grabbed a medium-sized bath towel instead of a hand towel. Now she's glad. Dark blue, ancient, and fraying at the ends, it's not something her mother will miss. She hacks off a strip about three inches wide, folds it in half, and stuffs it into her underwear. There's nothing to hold it in place, but she doesn't plan to move much today.

She shuffles onto the beach. All the dome tents from the night before have vanished, like a mushroom patch cleared by pickers. The bare expanse of silver-grey sand will be hers until early afternoon at least, while hikers travel west or east from the neighbouring campsites.

Black in silhouette, granite cliffs nose into the ocean at either end of the crescent beach. The water is a clear, dark turquoise, with crushed white clam shells underfoot. As the sky clears, the day is turning bright. The sun presses down between her shoulder blades like a warm hand. At the western end of the beach, a waterfall cascades off the edge of a cliff. That must be the "shower" the girl told her about yesterday. It sparkles in a welcoming way. She'll rinse herself off and then retrieve her food from the cache on her way back.

As she nears the waterfall, her skin tingles. She shucks off her clothes and runs into it. *Brr.* The water falls in clumps, not in an even flow. Freezing cold. But so refreshing. She massages the water through her hair and scrubs her arms and legs. With an automatic glance up and down the beach, she bends over, nose to knees, so that the water can rinse her bum and her genitals.

Her teeth are chattering by the time she steps out of the waterfall. She shakes all over the way a dog does after swimming. With the remains of her bath towel, she wipes herself down and then pulls her shorts and shirt back on.

The empty stretch of beach seemed peaceful just minutes ago. Now it seems spooky. It's so wide and so deserted. A cougar could be watching her from the trees.

She shakes her head to clear it. The cache is just ahead. She jumps off a log and scrambles up the path.

She gives a jolt when she sees a skinny young guy with a stringy mop of brown hair, rifling through her red fabric food sac. "Hey! That's my food!" She leaps onto the platform and grabs her bag.

He gasps and makes to dart away, but she seizes his arm.

"Let go of me!"

"Just hang on. Don't you have any food of your own?"

He scowls. "Where would I get food? You see a grocery store around here?" He wrenches himself free of her grip.

He's wearing cargo pants and a long sleeved t-shirt with holes at the cuffs. His running shoes aren't heavy enough for the trail. His face is streaked with dirt and bits of dried food. Twigs are caught in his hair, which is forming into matted clumps. He's jittery, shaking lightly all over. He flicks his hair off his face.

*He looks more like a homeless kid than a hiker. What's he doing out here alone?*

He eyes her bag. His legs quiver like he's dying to break into a run, but his gaze doesn't leave the bag of food. Just then his stomach growls.

Brooke doesn't have much appetite yet, but the boy is obviously famished. She says casually, "I'm about to cook up some dried lasagna. It serves two. Would you like some?"

He licks his lips but doesn't smile. "What's the catch?"

"You stop taking my food. I'll share with you, but I need some of it for myself. Deal?"

He looks at the ground and says nothing.

"I'm going to head back to my campsite and cook this up. Come by if you feel like it."

# CHAPTER 13

# seth: fair Trade

*Unbelievable.* Sure, last night raiding the cache was risky with all of the campers around. But this morning, he'd ignored his hunger pangs and forced himself to wait until the beach was deserted. Anything left behind in the food cache should have been fair game. He's already culled a blue tarp, a lighter, and a water bottle from the abandoned campsites.

Seth climbs up to the ridge that overlooks the beach, his surveillance position. It's not a long climb, but by the top his legs feel shaky and weak. He leans forward on his thighs, breathing heavily.

He scans the beach. There she is, setting up her stove on top of a log. Her tent is almost completely hidden in a treed alcove. That explains why he didn't see her earlier.

She lights the stove and sets a pot on top of it. She paces, half-stooped, pressing her hand into her lower back. *Is she looking for something on the ground?* It's hard to see her face from here, but she seems to be scowling. Probably pissed that she has to share her food with him. The weird thing is, she seems really familiar. *Does she go to my school?*

Steam is billowing out from under the pot lid — she's going to lose all her water. Seth almost yells down to warn her, but just then she turns her head and swoops in to rescue the pot from the stove. How she's going to turn a pot of creek water into lasagna, he has no idea.

She sits down on the log with her back to him. He ducks and dodges, trying to get a clearer view, but whatever she's doing in her lap remains a mystery. Seth pictures his dad's lasagna — its rich tomato and meat sauce; thick, wavy noodles; and melted, chewy, mozzarella cheese. His mouth waters, and before he can even make a decision, his feet carry him down the cliff.

The log that she's using as a kitchen counter stands about four feet high. A shiny plastic bag sits on the log next to the single-burner camp stove. There's no food in sight. And the girl has vanished, too.

Seth creeps closer to the log. The lettering on the plastic bag reads, "Mountain Meal: Italian Lasagna." The bag is warm to the touch. It's sealed with a zip lock top.

He lifts the bag, and it's heavy. Has she poured the water inside it? A spoon is crusted with something red that might be dried tomato sauce. He picks up the spoon and licks it. Salty.

He opens the bag. He can't help himself. Steam curls out, smelling of cheese and ground beef. He digs in the spoon and shovels crunchy noodle bits and soupy sauce into his mouth. He eats so fast, he barely chews the food before it slides into his stomach.

A moan rises up from behind the log. Seth shuffles sideways. The girl is down on all fours, propped on her knees and her elbows, her hands clasped in a fist under her forehead. Her butt faces Seth. She rocks forward and back. *Is it some sort of yoga move?*

"What are you doing?"

She twists to face him and sits cross-legged. "Hey, that's not ready yet!"

Seth cringes, feeling guilty. But his hunger is bigger than he is. And what's this girl going to do to him, anyway, besides chew him out? He shrugs. "Tastes okay to me."

Her face scrunches up, and she collapses on her back.

Seth's heart lurches. Did he upset her that much? "You all right?"

She groans. He's silent for a minute, but he can't stop chewing. He should probably save some food for her, but she looks pretty sick. Maybe she's lost her appetite. When his mom gets sick, she doesn't eat for a week. Getting the flu is the best crash diet, she says. "You going to want some of this lasagna?"

She doesn't answer. Instead, she breathes deeply, sucking in air past her teeth and blowing it slowly back out. Seth forces himself to stop eating. Finally, she says, "You can have it."

He exhales gratefully.

"But let's do a trade," she says.

"Name your price."

"Can you help me out today, like if I need water or something? I'm in a lot of pain here."

"Done."

Seth wonders what the problem is. There's no obvious sign of injury. *Migraine? Appendicitis?*

She gasps and rolls into a ball on her side, clutching her stomach.

*Duh. It's got to be her period.*

She drags herself up and staggers the few feet to her tent.

Seth hurries to her side and holds her arm to steady her. After he helps her inside the tent, he paces the beach in front of the campsite. His blood-sugar level has soared. He feels strong and ready for anything. But he's not sure what more he can do to help. Then it hits him: when he's feeling sick, a cold cloth on his forehead does wonders.

He kicks off his shoes and wades into the bay. He strips off his t-shirt and dips it into the cold salt water.

The girl is sleeping with her head near the opening of the tent. Seth squats to watch her upside-down face. Now he knows why she seems familiar. She looks like the picture he drew in his mind of his birth mom. Her brown-black hair and tanned skin make her look a little bit like him. Mainly, she's young and healthy, with a peaceful face. No frown lines. She's not old and bitter and full of regrets about how her life has turned out. Not full of anger at Seth, who she blames for driving her husband away. Not so desperate for a man that she dates a beer-guzzling bully and turns a blind eye when he targets her son.

The girl's chest rises and falls. Seth leans forward and grazes the damp t-shirt against her forehead. She reaches up her hand and brushes his wrist. Her eyelids flutter open. When she sees him, her pupils dilate, and she jerks her legs.

"It's a cold cloth," he says.

She pats the cloth and raises it up from her forehead so she can see what it's made of. She twists her head and her eyes drop to his bare chest. "Is this your t-shirt?"

Seth shrugs one shoulder and scratches his chest.

She lets her head sink back down. "Wow. I can't believe you did that."

"It's no big deal."

Seth feels awkward now that she's awake. She sniffs. As he glances down at her, she wipes her eyes. *Is she crying?*

"Now that you're awake, you can hold this yourself." He lets go of the t-shirt and squats back on his heels. "When it gets too warm, tell me, and I'll dip it in the ocean again."

"Thanks. I mean it. That's the nicest thing someone's done for me in . . . practically forever." She smacks her lips. "Can you pass me my water?"

"Don't push your luck."

Her eyebrows shoot up in surprise.

"Kidding!"

She tries to swat him with the t-shirt.

"Hey! Don't mess with the compress!"

Seth fetches the water bottle from the "kitchen," rapping under his breath. "I said, don't mess with the compress, baby! Don't mess with the compress."

From the way she's biting her lips, the girl is trying not to laugh at him. *Great, she thinks I'm an idiot.* Stung, Seth shuts up.

She strains to lift her neck up and swallows some water, dribbling a bit down her chin. She sets the bottle next to her foamie. "I'm going to need some privacy in a minute."

"Trying to get rid of me?"

"Just for a bit."

"That's cool. I've got somewhere to be."

Seth aims for the cliff at the end of the beach. Climbing up it and scaling back down on the other side will take him to the cove where he spent the night.

"Hey!"

He turns back. "Yeah?"

"Where are you going?"

"Like I said, I have somewhere to be."

She seems to be watching an ant climb up the lip of her tent. She flicks the tent from the inside. "What I mean is, there's going to be another batch of campers arriving soon, and I'm not really in the mood to be social. Do you know of another place to camp close by?"

He feels paralyzed. He's not sure how far he can trust her.

She doesn't wait very long before calling, "Never mind. See you later."

*That's a relief.* He tosses his head and scrambles up the cliff.

# CHAPTER 14

# Brooke: Burial

Brooke pulls herself out of the tent and hobbles into the bushes, wincing. She's never had cramps this bad. *Is it from the hardcore exercise yesterday? How do girls in adventure sports cope?* She has to bury the blood-soaked scrap of towel before it attracts predators. Bears and cougars. Maybe birds of prey, too. Vultures, for sure, with their red beaks and disturbing habit of circling.

She kneels and pats the ground until she finds a stick. With a pointy end, she chips at the dirt. A stick isn't the greatest tool, and she keeps hitting rocks and roots. When the stick breaks, she feels around until she finds a thicker one. She gouges into the earth over and over until, finally, a shallow hole opens up. It's hard to make it any deeper — the ground gets harder and rockier the further down she digs. She reaches inside her underwear and scoops out the towel, pinching the ends together. It drops to the bottom of the hole with a plop. She slides the scooped-out earth back over the hole and pats it into place.

She sits back on her heels and clasps her elbows. The pile of dirt looks like a burial mound, a gravesite for a small cat or a bird. Or something even smaller.

Maybe it really *is* a grave. Maybe the cramps are so intense because it's a *miscarriage*, not a period. If there *was* a potential being inside, she might have killed it by hiking so hard! A weight presses on the centre of her chest. She digs her fingernails into her palms.

Until the past few days, the link between fooling around with Adam and — well, a baby — seemed abstract. Pregnancy was a distant threat, kind of like the chance of getting killed in a car accident. Sure, it could happen, but only paranoid people let it stop them from driving.

She catches the flaw in her own logic. *It might be paranoid to avoid driving altogether. But it's rational to take precautions, like observing the speed limit and wearing a seatbelt.*

Or using birth control.

Her shoulders shake with sobs. She's had such a close call. She makes a promise to herself: *This won't happen again.* She'll make changes, like break up with Adam, or get a prescription for the Pill.

A gush between her legs pulls her back to the present. She needs to make more rags that she can rinse in the ocean and hang up to dry. *No more graves.*

She slices off two more strips from her towel and then wades into the ocean in her underwear and t-shirt. If she can bear to submerge herself to the waist, she can rinse off and feel a little cleaner.

Goosebumps break out on her arms and legs. The water looks glassy and inviting, but it's freezing cold. When it reaches her knees, she can't go any further. The bones in her feet ache, and her calves are going numb. She ties her t-shirt in a knot at her waist, and then she squats to submerge her hips. She stretches out the crotch of her underwear and splashes icy water through the inch-wide gap.

By the time her sponge bath is over, a new troop of backpackers is arriving at the west end of the beach. The bright colours of their windbreakers match the cheerful tone of their voices, which carry across the water. In her sombre mood, Brooke can't stand the thought of meeting groups of people and making conversation. Maybe she can follow that guy who was helping her. He's probably found a quiet place to spend the night. He seems to be avoiding crowds, too. Water sloshes against her shins as she hurries back to shore.

At her campsite, she changes into dry underwear and stuffs it with a clean rag. She pulls on her dirty hiking pants. It takes her under five minutes to roll up her sleeping bag and take down her tent. In five more, she has packed everything, including the empty bag of lasagna, into her backpack. Her wet underwear hangs from a strap on the outside of her pack alongside the guy's soggy t-shirt. *I've got to get that back to him. Besides, it's a good excuse to find him.*

As she heads in the direction the guy has gone, she pauses to glance at the burial mound. The relief she felt at first when her period started has changed into something more complicated. There's a nagging ache in the middle of her chest, a mixture of sadness and guilt. She's going to have to carry it around — unless she can walk it off.

She scales the bluff at the end of the beach to find a dense patch of woods. There's hardly a trail at all, more of a trace, just wide enough to pass through. The bluff stretches ten metres across. On the far side, it drops practically straight back down to a sliver of beach. Brooke hesitates on the edge of the cliff. Halfway down, granite gives way to earth, and a narrow ridge descends to the shore.

She inches down, the weight of the pack dragging at her. She skids. The soles of her hiking boots have little grip on the bare rock. She crouches on her heels and her pack pulls her onto her bum. The pack weighs as much as a two-year-old child and seems to have a will of its own. At any moment, she might land flat on her back, and — helpless as a tortoise — slip and spin to her death. She unbuckles the waist and chest straps, shrugs off the pack, and lets it bounce and roll to the beach. It lands just clear of the water. Free of her pack, she picks her way down, like Spider-Man, almost floating.

At the bottom, she breathes deeply. The tension across her shoulders melts away. She unlaces her boots, stretches out on the sand with her pack for a pillow, and shuts her eyes

# CHAPTER 15

# seth: rescue

The tide comes in faster than you'd think. In minutes, the girl will be underwater. He's been keeping his eye on her and letting her sleep as long as he can, but her time is up. "Hey." Seth nudges her with his toe. "The tide's coming in."

"Mm." She rubs her eyes. "So?"

Just then a wave splashes the soles of her feet. She scrambles to shove her feet back into her boots and stand up.

The incoming tide surges with an angry-sounding thud. Seth jumps up onto a log. He reaches down to grab the girl's pack and hoists it up beside him. The water licks her feet, and she hops up to join him on the log.

"It looks like this beach is going to be under water tonight," he says. He turns his head to the point that juts out to the left. "While you were sleeping, I scoped out a better site."

"Really?" The way the girl raises her voice at the end of the word makes her sound desperate.

The sea sloshes against the base of the log. "Look, we need

to get going." He's not sure it's smart to bring her with him, but he can't just leave her to drown. "You up for it?"

She looks really worn out, but she nods.

"Follow me." The cliffs that lead to the point look sheer, but they taper slightly at the bottom into a rock skirt. It's just wide enough to travel on. "Watch your step. It can be slick."

The waves keep tossing themselves against the point. Seth gets soaked to the ankle and leans into the wall. He pauses, one hand gripping a nub of rock, and looks over his shoulder. The girl is trailing far behind. *Her heavy pack.* Of course, that makes it much harder. Also, more dangerous. If she slips, the pack will drag her down.

She raises her head. Her face looks green. She must be really scared. Seth gives her the thumbs up and shouts, "You're doing great!" He waits for her to get closer before he starts scrambling again.

When they finally round the point, a small rocky beach flashes in the next cove. Seth walked across it the day before on his way to Bear Beach. It's broad enough to give them shelter at high tide. If they keep picking their way along the point, they should just make it to the beach before the tide covers up their footholds.

Just as he jumps off the rock and lands in a crouch on the beach, a scream sounds behind him, followed by a splash. He pulls himself upright and turns around. The girl flounders in the water. He doesn't know how deep it is.

She seems to struggle to her feet, but she gets knocked back down again by the next wave. Her waterlogged pack must weigh a ton. He's got to go help her.

He kicks off his shoes, strips off his jacket and pants, and throws them higher up the beach. As he wades into the water, sharp rocks drive into the soles of his feet. He gasps and lifts one knee in the air. The girl keeps flailing. It looks like she's having trouble getting the pack off. He shuts out the pain in his feet and plunges into the water.

*Damn, it's cold.* Seth knows how to dogpaddle, but he can't swim well. The tide keeps surging.

He wades deeper and deeper. The water is so cold, his heart hammers. He's up to his nipples by the time he reaches her. Being numb protects him for now. He reaches for her shoulders to steady her. The chest strap is already floating free. She fumbles to undo the belt buckle at her waist. With Seth's help, she drops the pack and stands free. He hooks a strap in his elbow. The pack is heavy, but it floats. He backs up, and the tide pushes him toward the shore. He can almost ride the waves, the pack bumping along behind him.

The girl follows. They make it to the beach at the same time, and together they carry the pack up above the high water mark. It's got to weigh fifty pounds by now. They both grunt as they drop it on the pebbles.

"What a disaster!" She sounds angry, like it's his fault she fell in the water.

"You didn't have to follow me."

"I'm not blaming you. God! You just saved my life, practically." Her lungs heave as she catches her breath. "I don't even know your name."

"It's Seth." He's suddenly conscious of standing there wearing only wet underwear. He looks around for his clothes.

"I'm Brooke." She sneezes. "I have to try and dry this stuff out." She unzips her pack and starts to yank out the contents.

Seth pulls on his dry jacket and wraps his arms across his

chest. "Too bad we're not closer to the hot spring."

"Hot spring?" Brooke stares at him, a soaked towel dangling from her hand.

"Yeah. It's pretty close to Mystic Beach, I think."

She shakes her head as she wrings out the towel. "There's no hot spring anywhere along the Juan de Fuca trail. Not according to the guidebook."

It's Seth's turn to gawk. *But it saved my ass when I fell in the ocean.* A shudder passes over his body. *Was it all a dream?* He pushes up his left sleeve and lifts his arm to his face. A faint smell of sulphur rises from his skin. *It must have been real.* But now isn't the time to argue with her.

It takes them an hour to spread everything out, including Seth's underwear and t-shirt. "Needed to do laundry anyway," he jokes. The afternoon sun is shining directly on them, and he's warm enough for now in his dry pants and jacket.

Brooke is wearing shorts and a tank top while she waits for her outer clothes to dry. She sits down with a log for a backrest and picks up her water bottle. "Crap! I'll need more water than this to make us something to eat."

*Seth to the rescue. Again.* "If you give me your bottle, I can find some."

"Okay. Then I'll make us some chili for dinner."

Seth looks at the stove. "Is that thing going to light after being in the ocean?"

"It was in a zip-lock bag along with the matches. So I think it will." She chafes her upper arm with the opposite hand and

73

then switches sides. "And this time, you have to leave me some. I'm starving."

"Deal."

Seth heads for a narrow creek he's spotted at the far end of the beach. Giving Brooke a hand actually makes him feel stronger. He's looking after himself, and not only that, he's helping to take care of someone else. It's the next best thing to having Patches around.

# CHAPTER 16

# Brooke: Adopted

Brooke wakes up in the pitch dark, shivering. Wind howls around the tent. The damp sleeping bag feels clammy against her. At least it has trapped some of her body heat. But Seth has got to be frozen. After they ate together, she invited him to share her tent, but he refused. She should find him and bring him back. She tries to move, but her limbs won't budge. Tiredness pins her to the ground. The wind blows an eerie lullaby, and she drifts back to sleep.

At daybreak, the sound of a zipper wakes Brooke up. Her heart trip-hammers. "Seth?"

The zipper stops. She sits up and opens it the rest of the way to poke her head out. Seth is crouched beside her tent, blowing on his hands.

"Are you all right? You look frozen."

Seth's lips are blue. "I need to go. To warm up." He blurts out the words from between chattering teeth. "Didn't want to leave. Without telling you."

"Wait!" Brooke drops the tent flap and grabs her clothes from the bottom of her sleeping bag. They're warm from her body heat and only slightly damp. She tunnels her limbs into them and zips herself into her jacket. She calls through the doorway of the tent. "Seth, why don't you get inside my sleeping bag and warm up?"

She flips open the door flap and comes nose to nose with Seth. His jaw has dropped, though it's still jiggling as his teeth chatter. Brooke rolls her eyes at his shocked expression. "*By yourself,* I mean." She brushes past him, sliding her feet into her hiking boots and giving him a nudge. "Go on. I'll heat up some water while you do that."

Brooke picks her way down the rocky beach to the creek. The wind has died down, and the ocean stretches out smooth as a grey satin sheet. She squats to fill up her water bottle and camp pot. A few twigs and pine needles float on the surface of the water. She empties the containers and fills them again, but it's the same each time. *Oh well.* A little plant matter won't hurt anyone.

Next, she rinses out the towel scrap in her underwear and replaces it with one that's damp but clean. *Ugh. I'll never take a tampon for granted again.* She tests her quads by pushing to standing. Her thighs don't scream like they did yesterday. Her abdominal cramps haven't returned, either — not yet, anyway. She feels stronger.

Back at the tent, Brooke retrieves her single burner stove from its zip-lock bag and screws it into the can of propane that forms its base. She creates a flat surface on the side of a log by propping a rock underneath the bottom of the can. She twists a plastic knob on the side of the can to turn on the gas. With her thumb, she flicks the spring-loaded starter. An orange flame shoots up, and she turns it down to a steady blue glow.

When the rising bubbles make the pot slide, she holds the handle. "One one thousand, two one thousand, three one thousand . . ." Counting the seconds, she lets the water boil for three minutes to kill any parasites. Then she pours half the water from the pan into a cup. She rips open an instant oatmeal packet and stirs it in. "Seth, I've made you some hot oatmeal."

In the doorway of the tent, Seth sits up with the sleeping bag pulled to his armpits. "This thing is like a furnace!" He takes the cup of oatmeal. "Thank you."

"Do you want some tea?" Brooke drops a teabag into the pot to steep in the leftover water. "When you've finished the oatmeal, I'll have to pour it into the same cup. That's the only one I have."

By the time Seth finishes his tea, he's no longer shivering, and his teeth have stopped chattering. Colour is returning to his lips. "What are your plans for today?" he asks.

Brooke is boiling a second pot of water for her own breakfast. "I need to get back. My family must be getting worried."

A shadow crosses Seth's face. "Right."

"You're welcome to walk with me. Or even . . ." She wants to offer him a ride into town, but she holds back from saying it. By the time they get to the car, he might trust her enough to go with her. "What do you think?"

Seth shrugs. "I've got nothing better to do."

Once she's eaten and packed up her gear, they scale the cliff to the forest. No sense risking another fall into the ocean, even though the tide has ebbed. Seth leads the way and Brooke follows on his heels. "How long are you going to stay out here, Seth?"

He shrugs. "Probably keep it up for the summer."

"What about your parents?"

He snorts. "What about them?" He flings a stick he's been carrying out to sea. "Only thing I miss is my dog." The stick bobs on the choppy water.

She pictures a dog trotting next to Seth and fetching sticks when he throws them. It looks right. "Is that a reason to go, um, home, then?"

"Hell no! Dad took my dog when he moved out. I hardly ever see him."

So his parents split up, and he lost his dog. There's got to be more to the story. Brooke fiddles with the chest strap of her pack. "If your parents don't know you're out here, they're probably sick with worry."

"Doubt it," Seth says. "I'm sure Mom thinks I'm at Dad's. Dad assumes I'm with Mom." He grunts, and his next words come out in a dark, strained voice that Brooke hasn't heard him use before. "Only one who might suspect the truth is King A-hole. Mom's new squeeze."

*That sounds like trouble.*

Seth grabs another stick, breaks it over his knee, and throws each piece away, really hard. They pinwheel down to the water.

Brooke wracks her mind for something to say to console

the guy. They trek almost vertically, taking small steps, and searching for foot and handholds in the bushes and plants. The dull colours of his clothes blend into the landscape, but the bright blue tarp poking out of his pack makes him easy to spot.

As they crest a ridge, she hoists herself up beside him. "Can we sit down? I need a little rest." The cramps have held off today, but her back still aches. And even if she were feeling one hundred percent, this would still be a strenuous hike.

He shrugs. "Whatever."

She breathes until her heart slows. "I came out here to escape from my family too, you know. From my mom, anyhow."

He raises an eyebrow. "Yeah?" From his flat tone of voice, it's clear he doesn't think there's any comparison between her life and his.

She shifts on the ground uncomfortably. Hopefully, they'll cross a creek soon, so she can rinse out her towel scrap. She takes a deep breath. "When I was younger, I used to get really mad at my parents. At my mom, anyway. She was always so uptight. She always tried to stop me having fun. So to get revenge, I'd imagine I was adopted. I figured my real parents had to give me up because they were so young. But they wanted to keep me all along. They loved me so much."

She has been staring at a fern, not really seeing it as her childhood fantasy plays in her head. She plucks off a frond and chews the end. "I don't know. It seemed to help."

The hungry look on Seth's face startles her. Raw longing. His eyes mist over, and he looks at the ground.

The frond drops from her lips. "Did I say something wrong?"

He grips the trunk of a slender fir tree and raises his head. "I'm adopted."

She shifts to face him. "I'm sorry."

"And you —" He cuts himself off and turns his head away.

"Yeah?" Brooke touches his shoulder.

Seth's shoulder twitches under her hand. "You remind me of her."

Brooke isn't sure she's heard him right. *Who is "her"?* She lifts her hand off his shoulder and waits until he glances at her. She juts her neck forward, eyebrows lifted in a question.

Seth shrugs one shoulder toward his ear, head tilted. "You know. My birth mom."

Brooke breathes in sharply. She would never have guessed. No one has ever told her that she reminds them of their mother. *It's ridiculous!*

She swallows her reaction. He averts his eyes and stands up, swivelling away from her.

Brooke hoists herself up and follows, but her cheeks are burning. *I almost had an unplanned pregnancy. I could have been a teen mom. It might have been me giving up a child for adoption.*

*Does it show somehow?!*

# CHAPTER 17

# seth: fire

A few clicks into the hike, Seth is fading. It would have made a lot more sense to stay put. At night, he could have doubled back to poach food at Bear Beach. Brooke's supplies seem really low. Not to mention, he runs the risk of bumping into the park ranger now that they've joined the cleared path. It must be obvious that he's been sleeping in his clothes, and that means he owes camping fees.

The ground turns spongy underfoot. The trail levels off and broadens out for a kilometre or so. Brooke moves up until she's shoulder-to-shoulder with him. "Have you ever thought of contacting your birth parents?"

Seth's so surprised that he coughs. Being adopted isn't something he talks about. He's kept it a secret at school. His birth-mom fantasy has stayed tucked away in a private corner of his mind. When he's sad and alone, he unfolds it like a treasure and uses it to comfort himself.

But now that Brooke knows he's adopted, she has the power to bring it up. He's not in control any more. It's like she carries a piece of him.

"You don't want to talk about it?" she says.

*Way to state the obvious.*

"I'm sorry," she says.

Seth sighs. *Maybe it wouldn't hurt. Maybe it would be a relief.* "I tried to contact my birth mom." He puts on a nasal voice. *"We regret that adoptees under nineteen can't use our registry."* Anger pushes up inside him. It feels hot, like pus under a barely scabbed-over wound. His whole life has been run by Social Services. As far as they're concerned, he's just a few pieces of paper in a file folder. He has no rights.

He picks his way from one stone to the next across a small creek. He waits for Brooke on the opposite bank. The water churns at his feet.

She pushes off the bank and lands on a stone. "That sucks." She searches for the next foothold. "Do you know anything about them? Your birth parents, I mean?"

"Hardly anything." He turns and begins to climb the switchbacks out of the gully. At the next hairpin turn, he pauses with his hands on his hips. Red pine needles lie scattered over the moist dark earth. All of a sudden, he needs to empty his bowels. "I'll catch up to you in a minute, okay?"

Brooke squints at him. "Huh?"

Seth shuffles back down the hill, and when he passes her, he gives her a nudge from behind. "Go on."

He wades into a thick patch of salal and pulls down his pants just in time. Diarrhea squirts out. *What the hell?* He yanks leaves off the nearest bush and wipes as best he can.

When he drags himself back to the trail, Brooke is waiting thirty metres on, looking back in his direction. *She better not have seen anything.* He catches up to her, and she moves aside to let him pass. He shakes his head. "You set the pace for a while."

The runs hold off until they stop for lunch beside a stream. Seth dives into the woods again. When he gets back, Brooke is kneeling on the bank, pumping water. "How are you doing for water, Seth?"

"I could use some."

"How about lunch? I've still got some of these cheese sticks."

A wave of nausea washes over him at the thought. "No thanks."

"Or this veggie bacon. It's getting a little slimy, but it's still good. I smelled it."

Seth pales. He takes a step backward and sinks onto a log. He bends forward and props his forehead on the heels of his hands.

Brooke sets down the water pump and comes to his side. "Are you all right?"

He raises his head. "I'm fine."

Their eyes meet for a second. She's searching his face.

He looks away. "You just killed my appetite, that's all. Had a bad experience with veggie bacon a while back."

When she offers the water bottle, he swallows a few mouthfuls. He's thirsty, but his stomach feels queasy. "How far are you planning to go today?" Seth says.

"At first I was thinking China Beach," she says. "That's where I left my car."

Seth drops his chin to his chest. Part of him hopes she'll stay one more night, but he tries to fight the feeling down.

"I think my legs are done, though," she says. "I'm going to stop for the day at Mystic."

He lifts his head. The inside of his chest seems to expand like an accordion. But he looks away and stops himself from smiling.

As soon as they spill out of the trail onto Mystic Beach, Brooke drops her pack and claims a spot. Further east, a large group has set up a communal site. Several metres west lies a ring of stones that contains the remains of a fire. *Sure could have used a fire last night.* Seth shivers at the memory. It might be warmer to camp in the forest tonight, and it would definitely be more private.

He climbs back up the bank into the woods and searches out a fallen tree. Tying the tarp to its branches and using the side of the log as a wall, he rigs up a shelter. He crawls into it and smoothes the ground into a floor. He sets down his pack. *Not bad.* He's almost getting used to living in the woods.

As he makes his way back to the beach, he gathers all the fallen branches he can find. Luckily, it hasn't rained in a while, so the wood is pretty dry. The fire ring holds some ashy, half-burnt pieces that can serve as kindling. Seth kneels on the sand and props up the fresh wood. He's started a lot of fires, but never without paper. If only he had some — even one sheet.

*The letter.* He pulls it out of his pocket. The paper is warped, but it has dried out since his fall into the ocean. As he unfolds the sheet of paper, it dawns on him. *Today's my birthday.* It's a perfect time to burn this letter, with its screwed-up rules about how he can't contact his birth mom.

He balls it up, jams it under the wood, and lights it. He carefully blows on the flames until the fire catches. He adds bigger and bigger pieces of wood until he can sit back on his heels for a while and enjoy it.

He has been so focused on building the fire, he forgot about Brooke. He turns his head. Just a stone's throw away, she sits cross-legged in front of a tea candle. One hand rests on her heart, and her eyes are closed.

*What's she doing? Making a birthday wish? Too weird.*

Seth treads softly so as not to startle her. She doesn't hear him, so he stands there until it starts to feel like he's intruding on something private. He clears his throat. "What's up?"

# CHAPTER 18

# Brooke: Player

Brooke jumps at the sound of Seth's voice. She has been trying to pray for the spirit of a tiny being that may or may not have existed. One that she definitely wasn't ready to nurture but still feels sad about losing. *If it was even there in the first place.*

"Damn, you move quietly." She stares at the candle flame.

"Survival skill."

She bristles. *He sounds like Adam.* "What is it with you boys and your survival skills?"

Seth shrugs. "I don't know what you mean by 'you boys.' I'm the only one standing here."

"My boyfriend talks like that, too."

"I don't know what his deal is. But I learned how to creep around so I wouldn't get the shit kicked out of me."

Brooke slumps forward. "I'm sorry."

He squats beside her and clasps his wrist in one hand. He glances at the candle, then at her face. When he speaks again, his voice is softer. "What's the candle for?"

"It's kind of personal."

"Oh." Seth straightens up. "Well, I made a fire. I thought you might want to come and warm up."

A few metres beyond Seth, a blazing orange fire pops and cracks. Brooke blows out her candle and follows him down the beach.

She spreads her hands in front of the flames. "You sure know how to make a good fire."

Seth coughs. "Another survival skill. It meant I could stay outside all day and not have to deal with my mom."

"Which one?"

"My adoptive mom."

Brooke watches him. "Did she beat you?"

Seth keeps his eyes on the fire. "The beating happened in foster care." The sharp bones of his profile are softened by his downcast eyes and tucked chin. "Mom didn't hit me, but she'd attack in other ways. Whenever my dad was gone, it was pretty brutal."

"Couldn't you report her for that?"

Seth raises his head like it weighs a hundred pounds and brushes his hair out of his face. He looks her in the eye. "And get sent back to foster care?" He shows more strength and sadness than anyone his age should have to.

"I'm so sorry, Seth."

He collapses onto a log, chin in his hands, hair hiding his face. They both watch the fire. Healing warmth radiates from the flames as the branches slowly turn to ash. After a long pause, Seth clears his throat. "You know what day it is today?"

Brooke starts. It takes a moment for her eyes to refocus on Seth's face. "Actually, no, I don't." She chuckles at how easy it is to lose track of days of the week on the trail.

He shakes his hair off his forehead. He rests his elbows on

his thighs, his hands hanging loose between his knees. The sad look in his hazel eyes pierces her. "It's my birthday."

"Really? Why didn't you say so before? Happy birthday!"

Seth's face grows longer as he stares at the fire. "I always wonder if she thinks of me on this day."

"Who?"

"Who do you think?" He doesn't say *you idiot*, but his tone of voice implies it.

Brooke bites her lip. "Of course. Your birth mom."

He picks up a stick and pokes the fire. "She'll be thirty-two by now."

Brooke raises her eyebrows. "Really?" She tries to do the math in her head. "So how old was she when she had you?"

"Subtle, Brooke." Seth twists his mouth into a sour expression. "Why don't you come right out and ask me how old I am instead of trying to trick me into telling you?"

Brooke isn't thinking of Seth, though. She's wondering about the girl who gave birth to him.

"I'm sixteen," he says.

"Oh."

"Same age she was when she had me."

"Wow." *She was two years younger than me. Just a kid. But she went through with it. She carried the baby to term and gave birth and here he is. Almost grown up already.*

"That's so . . . young."

Seth shakes his head. "It doesn't *feel* that young. Believe me."

If young means happy and carefree, then Seth has a point. He doesn't seem that young.

They fall silent and watch the fire burn down.

"It freaked me out when you were sitting by the candle," Seth says.

"What do you mean?"

"I thought it was a birthday candle."

A chill rises off the sand, and Brooke shudders. *He's marking his birth while I'm marking a death. A possible death.* She keeps her eyes on the fire.

"It wasn't though, right?"

"Hm?" She glances at Seth, who's studying her face. "No. I'm not psychic!" He seems to be waiting for an explanation. "It was a prayer candle, I guess."

"What were you praying for?"

She sighs, hoping he'll drop the subject.

"Come on, I told you mine, you have to tell me yours."

"Okay." She crosses her arms in front of her chest. "I came out here thinking I might be pregnant because my period was late. When I started bleeding, I didn't know for sure if it was a period or a — a miscarriage." She takes a deep breath. "Just in case, I was lighting a candle for the —" Her voice cracks. She shakes her head. "If there *was* something there, then what if all the intense hiking was just too much? I could have . . ."

Seth's mouth hangs open for five full seconds. Then his features start to twist. He springs to his feet and swings his head from side to side as if he's looking for something to pick up and hurl.

"What is it?" she says.

"I can't believe I felt sorry for you!" He kicks sand on the fire and stamps on the burning logs. "Baby-killer!" The logs break into charred fragments under his feet.

"But I don't even know for sure if I was pregnant."

He glares at her. "You should have found out! You wouldn't have even had to give the baby up for adoption because you're what, twenty?"

"Eighteen."

"Same difference. You're evil! I hope you *never* get to be a mother!" He picks up a smouldering piece of wood and flings it toward the ocean. He pitches one piece after another until the wood is gone and only the circle of stones remains where the fire has been.

He finally stands still and locks eyes with her. "I can't believe I trusted you."

He turns on his heel and vanishes into the bush.

# CHAPTER 19

# seth: secrets

Seth runs to the lean-to he has made with the tarp and throws himself under it. He clutches his backpack to his chest and curls into a ball. Of all the horrible memories Brooke could have stirred up, she's picked one of the worst.

It happened the day he left foster care, right before the Migliozzis picked him up. His half-brother Keith told him a story that he's tried to forget ever since. It has to be a lie because otherwise it blots out his birth-mom fantasy. They can't both be true.

Twigs snap under someone's feet. *Has she followed him? Damn her!*

"Seth?" Brooke calls.

He doesn't answer.

She steps a few feet closer. "Seth? Are you in there?"

His intestines seize up, and a moan escapes from his lips. Footsteps crunch toward the tarp, and Brooke lifts up a corner to peer in. "Get away from me!"

An almost empty water bottle has slid to his feet. She picks it up, unscrews the cap, and sniffs. She makes a face. "You haven't been treating your water, have you?"

"What's it to you?"

"All those times you dropped behind me on the trail today . . . was that because of diarrhea?"

He doesn't answer.

"And the way you looked so pale and nauseous at lunch. You might have Beaver Fever!"

He shuts his eyes. "What's that?" Drops of sweat bead on his forehead from the pain of the cramps.

"It's caused by a parasite in the water that comes from animal feces. It can make you really sick and last for months."

"Lovely."

Brooke squats on her heels and pulls her drinking bottle out of her pack. "This is treated water." She takes a long swallow from her bottle and passes it to Seth. "You can keep it."

He doesn't like accepting anything from her, but he's thirsty. He props himself up so that a log supports his neck and shoulders. He takes the bottle, lifts his head, and swallows.

"I know I upset you with what I said," she says.

Seth chokes on the water and shakes his head. "You upset me with what you *did*." He wipes his mouth with the back of his hand.

"I admit I made mistakes." Brooke keeps her eyes on his face. "And I won't let the same thing happen again."

Seth uses his most sarcastic voice. "Good for you." He hopes she'll take the hint and scram, but she keeps looking at him, her eyes filled with something that looks like pity. He'll have to get rid of her another way. He fakes a wince, as if his guts are cramping up again. "You got your pack with you?"

She nods.

"These cramps are getting worse. It's only a couple of clicks to the parking lot, and we still have an hour or so of daylight. Maybe you could take me in to a clinic tonight."

Her eyes bug, but she recovers and nods. "Sure thing."

Soon they're travelling toward the trailhead. Even though he's feeling weak, Seth moves more easily than Brooke since his pack is so much lighter than hers. At the crest of a steep hill, when Brooke is winded, Seth says, "I need some privacy."

"What do you mean?"

Seth shoots her a look. "What do you *think* I mean?"

She turns her back, and he picks a path through the bush. With a five-to-ten-minute lead, he should be able to lose her for good. She's like sand in an eyeball, irritating him to the point of tears.

He treads lightly so that the sound of cracking twigs doesn't give him away, but it slows down his progress. Before long, snapping and cracking sounds rise up behind him. She's *running* after him. He never thought she'd drop her pack to chase him!

He breaks into a run, too, heading for the sound of flowing water. He glances back. *She's gaining on him.*

He fords a stream, hoping she won't want to follow him if it means getting her boots wet. On the far side, he hunches over, hands on his knees.

She halts at the stream across from him and rests her hands on her hips, chest heaving. "What's going on?"

"Changed my mind," he says between gasps.

"You could die out here!"

"I don't know why someone who just killed her baby should care."

Seth collapses onto the ground. He feels limp with fatigue. Brooke sits cross-legged on the opposite bank. They both catch their breath as the stream gushes past between them. After a long pause, Brooke responds. "At the very worst, it was a miscarriage. And I do feel bad about it." She tries to make eye contact, but he won't hold her gaze. "I just don't get why it bothers *you* so much."

Seth's forehead sinks even lower until it's almost touching his shins. When he speaks again, he's whispering. "I was in foster care with my half-brother."

"I can barely hear you."

Seth raises his voice a little. "He said it was all my fault we were taken away from our dad." Seth pictures himself eavesdropping on the stairs. "One night I heard my foster mother talking to a friend of hers in the kitchen. She said, 'Seth would have been adopted long ago, but no one wants to take an older child like Keith.' Her friend said, 'And they have to keep them together?' My foster mother said, 'They try to, but it's a shame in this case. They're only half-brothers.' They must have decided to bend the rules in the end. I finally got adopted when I was seven."

"What happened to Keith?"

Seth shrugs. "He told me he was going back to our dad, but I didn't believe him. My foster mother said our dad couldn't stay clean." He grunts. "I used to wonder why they didn't just give him some soap."

He lowers his head, refocuses on the stream, and fidgets with a twig. It makes him feel naked to be exposing these old secrets. Another cramp rips through him. He clutches his abdomen and bends in half. "Agh!"

Brooke tries to leap across the stream, falls short, and drenches her feet. She pulls herself onto the bank beside him. "Are you okay? What's wrong?"

He answers through clenched teeth. "Cramps."

"This is nuts. We need to get you to a clinic."

Seth shakes his head.

"Come on, Seth. We're so close to the car."

He gasps for breath. "I know how to hitchhike, okay? Did it ever occur to you that I don't need your help?" The spasm passes, and he straightens up. "Right before I left the foster home, Keith said my birth mom tried to kill me when I was still inside her. He said our dad found her and took her to the hospital." Seth swallows. His voice catches in his throat. "Then I met you, and you reminded me of her — and you said you killed your . . ." He hiccups.

"Oh, Seth . . ."

"Keith said, 'I wish Dad let you die!' And right now I wish . . . I wish he had, too."

The moss-covered trees loom silent and still all around. Seth sniffs and wipes his face on his sleeve. "Now would you please just leave me alone?"

He expects her to argue, but she says, "It's getting dark. I have to go back for my gear. Will be you be okay here for now?"

Seth pulls the blue tarp out of his knapsack. "Of course I'll be okay."

"I'll come back as soon as I can."

As annoyed with her as he is, and as much as he doesn't feel like talking, he feels worse after she leaves. He rolls himself up in the tarp. The inside of his chest pulls taut as he tries to hold all the feelings in.

He has always told himself that Keith was lying, that his birth mom really loved him. Otherwise, why didn't Keith taunt him with the abortion story all along? Now the truth fills him with coldness. Keith was hoarding that secret like the powerful weapon it was. It must have been his worst fear that Seth would get to leave foster care without him. Up until the end, he must have hoped the Migliozzis would take him along, too. And when they didn't — he had nothing more to lose.

The gloom is thickening fast. He burrows deeper into his tarp to ward off the chill. *So I've been wrong to dream of my birth mom. She wanted me dead.* Through the limbs of a tree, he can just make out the glimmer of a star overhead. His adoptive mom wanted to change him, but at least she wanted him in the first place. Life with his adoptive parents — his life, period! — was actually a lucky break. No one wanted his brother. *Poor Keith.* After the adoption, Seth always turned down the chance to visit him. He'd be grown up by now, twenty-one. Maybe he should try to get in touch with him. Seth shivers. *Or maybe not. God knows what he's into these days.*

The rustling in the woods is probably just a couple of deer. But the steps sound too heavy, and they're getting closer.

"Seth, it's me!" Brooke calls out. "I'll pitch my tent over here."

He thought for sure she would camp on the beach. The band of tension in his chest relaxes a bit. He feels like apologizing, but instead, he says, "Okay." In a voice that's likely too soft to be heard over the sound of the creek, he adds, "Thanks for coming back."

# CHAPTER 20

# Brooke: payback

Brooke wriggles inside her sleeping bag. The bumpy forest floor pokes into her spine and hips, making it much less comfortable to lie on than the beach. Still, it's worth it to be near Seth. The tarp rustles as he shifts. She'd feel more useful if she could hold a cold cloth to his forehead like he did for her. But sleeping close to him is better than nothing.

She's still mulling over what he told her about his birth mom and how she tried to abort him. *How terrible for him.* What happened to Seth makes her see her own pregnancy scare in a different light. *It's truly a matter of life and death.*

A question still gnaws at her. It wasn't totally Adam's fault that she risked having unprotected sex. So why did she? It wasn't that she didn't know better. It wasn't even that she just got carried away. She chose to go along with it.

The answer bubbles up inside her, as if she's known it all along. It's the same reason she dated Adam in the first place: to rebel against her mom. After her mom forbade her to backpack with Adam last year, Brooke defied her at every chance she got. Maybe it wasn't always conscious, but she did it all the same. With Adam. With school. With work. Even now, with this solo backpacking trip.

A root or a rock is digging into her back. She turns onto her side to accommodate it. *Mom's not the enemy. We don't agree on much, but I can't just keep doing the opposite of what she wants all the time. I need to think things through. That's the only way to make a good decision.*

The stream burbles beside her as if it's responding to her thoughts. It keeps gushing all through the night.

At first light, the stirring of the tarp wakes her up. She pulls herself out of the sleeping bag and then the tent. Her body feels covered in bruises from sleeping on the ground.

Crouched by the stream, Seth is filling up the water bottle that she gave him. "What do you think you're doing?"

"What's the problem? I'm already infected."

Brooke is parched. "Give me my bottle back then."

He raises his eyebrows with a disbelieving grin and chucks it to her. With big gestures, she unzips a pocket of her backpack, retrieves the treatment pills, and drops one into the water. He rolls his eyes.

"We must be close to the parking lot," she says.

"About a click."

"You think you can make it that far?"

Seth cups his hands in the stream and splashes his face with water. "I don't know."

"Come on, Seth, you have to try. I'll help you."

He scowls. "Of course I can *make* it."

"Then what's the problem?"

He cups his hands in the stream again and drinks out of them. "I've got a right to stay out here."

There's a reason Brooke followed Seth last night. She wanted to find him before anyone else did. A park ranger, she's sure, would size up the situation at a glance and take charge. He'd make decisions and give orders. She wouldn't be surprised if he hauled Seth up the path and corralled him into an ambulance. Brooke doesn't want anyone to make Seth feel powerless like that. *But now what?*

As she watches Seth drink handfuls of untreated water, Brooke knows that she'll have to call the authorities. No matter what, she can't just step back and let him die. He's barely sixteen. And Beaver Fever can be treated. He'll be fine.

She thinks it through. If she calls 911, they'll send Search and Rescue. It may take a few days, but they'll find him.

*They'll hunt him down and trap him.* And if he knows he's being tracked, he might do something *really* self-destructive. He might throw himself off a cliff, or let himself get dragged out to sea before anyone can save him. It would be so much better if he would just come with her.

Seth sits down at the base of a tree, using its trunk as a back rest. The stream flows in front of him like a protective moat.

"What about Patches? Don't you want to see him?"

The ghost of a smile touches Seth's face.

"I bet he misses you."

Seth nods. "I bet he does."

"Maybe he's your real family, then. Maybe it starts there. You need to go back to be there for him." As she talks, Brooke can't help but remember her own old fantasies of belonging to a different family. She regrets them now. Her parents love her, and even when her mother tries to control her, she means well.

"Do you mind?" Seth says.

"What?" Brooke turns up her hands.

"I need to visit the latrine."

Brooke holds back a grunt of disgust. *Between his diarrhea and my period, we're quite a pair.* She turns her back, and he crawls away. The stream trickles past. No one would guess that the clear, bubbling water could wreak so much havoc on the human intestines.

Twigs crackle under footsteps, and Brooke jumps to her feet. Seth's making a break for it. She leaps across the stream and chases him. She catches him in a bear hug. She smells his sickness and doesn't let go. Her cheek brushes his filthy one.

Seth's body tenses against hers. He resists and tries to twist away. She holds on with all her strength until the tension collapses. His body shudders against hers. She holds him close and rocks him back and forth, back and forth. His face feels cold and wet on her neck.

"Why do you want to help me?" he says. "Why do you care?"

"Because you're worth it." In a parallel universe, she might have given birth to a boy like him. She pictures the "burial mound" back at Bear Beach and sighs. "Besides, I've got enough on my conscience already."

# CHAPTER 21

# Seth: Telling

Seth has never felt emptier. After two days straight of diarrhea and not eating, he's got nothing left inside of him. And somehow he's coughed up all the secrets he's been hauling around for years. He floats along like a dried-up husk as he follows Brooke to her car.

"I don't think I need the clinic," he says.

Brooke opens the trunk of her dust-covered Toyota and lays her pack down inside it. "How do you know the cramps won't come back?" She opens the passenger door for him. "You also need to call your parents." She pulls out her cell and turns it on. "No signal."

"What a shame."

They load into the car, and in half an hour, they're in the heart of Sooke. She pulls into the plaza where Seth bought pizza the first night.

"I'm dying for a coffee," Brooke says.

"I need a bathroom."

The white porcelain toilet in the coffee shop is so clean

that it gleams. He washes his face and hands in the sink. As the warm water hits his skin, it releases a smell of sulphur. *There's no way that hot spring was all in my mind.*

He joins Brooke at a round table about two feet in diameter. She passes him her phone.

"Don't you have people to call first?" he says.

"Seth, at this point, technically, I could get charged with kidnapping. If you don't call somebody right away, I'm going to have to turn myself in."

"Okay, okay." He dials his dad's cell number.

His dad answers right away. "Hello?"

"Hi."

"Seth, is that you?"

"Yeah." The phone chimes, warning him of a low battery.

"Where are you?"

Brooke is watching him. He points to the door and mouths "outside." She nods. He opens the door and steps onto a sunny sidewalk. "I'm in Sooke."

"How did you get way out there?"

"This great invention called the bus."

His dad takes a breath. "I called on your birthday, and your mom said you disappeared days ago."

Seth snorts. "I'm surprised she noticed."

There's a pause. His dad seems to be searching for words. "Look, I'm off today. Where should I meet you?"

"This girl I'm with —"

"You're with a *girl*?"

Seth laughs. "Not in that way. Anyway, she thinks I should see a doctor."

"Why? What's wrong?"

"Nothing serious. Maybe a touch of Beaver Fever."

His dad exhales loudly. "I'll meet you at the walk-in clinic in Sooke. It might take me an hour to get there."

Seth waves to Brooke, who's sipping her coffee in the window. She gets to her feet, and a moment later, she's standing beside him. "What now?"

He hands back the phone. One side of his mouth pulls up in a sheepish grin. "The clinic, I guess."

Brooke smiles as she pockets the phone. "I'll give you a ride."

Back in the car, Seth says, "By the way, I killed your phone battery."

"Really?" Brooke lifts her eyebrows. "I guess I'll just have to show up on my parents' doorstep."

"How do you think that'll go over?"

"I don't know. My stuff might be thrown in boxes and sitting on the lawn."

He chuckles. "Harsh."

"Yeah." Brooke starts the engine. "Either way, I can't freeload at home much longer."

"What about living with your boyfriend?"

Brooke glances in the rear-view mirror. "My soon-to-be ex-boyfriend?"

"You're breaking up with him?"

Brooke nods.

"Because of . . . what happened?" Seth looks down. The wrists of his jacket are blackened by smudges of charcoal.

"Partly." She idles at a stop sign, waiting for a break in the traffic. "But also, I need to focus on finding a job and making a solid plan for the future."

"Sounds heavy."

Brooke shrugs. "Kind of." She revs the engine and pulls

onto the road. "But it's exciting, too."

"If you need a place to crash, you could probably pitch your tent in my dad's backyard."

Brooke grins. "Thanks, I'll keep that in mind." She taps his arm. "*If* you take a bath."

"Look who's talking!"

"Are you calling me stinky?"

Seth shakes his head. "You said it, not me, sister."

At the clinic, the doctor confirms that Seth's symptoms point to giardia — Beaver Fever. Since they're pretty severe, she writes him a prescription. He pockets it to give to his dad.

Brooke buys bottled water for them both, and they find a bench where they can soak up the sun while they wait for Seth's dad. Before long, he pulls up in his black pick-up truck. Seth's heart leaps to see Patches propped up in the passenger seat. At the sight of Seth, the dog throws back his head and barks non-stop.

"I should get going." Brooke passes him a scrap of paper. "Text me, okay?"

He nods. "Thanks for everything."

"You too," Brooke says as she slips away.

His dad must have rolled straight out of bed. He's wearing sweatpants, and his wavy hair is standing up, the black streaked by a few white strands that Seth hasn't noticed before.

"Buddy!" his dad calls. "Come 'ere." As his dad folds him into a hug, his whiskers scrape Seth's cheek.

Seth breaks away to kneel on the pavement. He buries his face in Patches' neck.

"Do you want to get some breakfast? There's a restaurant up the way."

Seth scratches the dog behind the ears. "Did you miss me, boy?"

His dad clears his throat. "It has an outdoor patio, so Patches could stay with us."

Seth pats the dog and stands up. "Then let's go."

When they're settled at a table with Patches curled up on Seth's lap, the waitress arrives. She looks back and forth from Seth to his dad. "Coming in for the Father's Day special? We're offering it all week."

His dad winks at Seth. "Tell us about that."

"It's a two-for-one deal for fathers and their kids, and I'm guessing . . ." She glances from one to the other and smiles.

"Yep," his dad says. "We're father and son."

"I thought so! What would you like?"

While they're waiting for their food, Seth's dad sips coffee. "So are you going to tell me what this is all about?"

Seth flicks a glance at his dad. A few white whiskers show in his beard. Pouches have formed under his eyes. All of a sudden, he looks old and tired. But he doesn't look mean.

His dad was never mean.

Just absent. Distracted. Clueless.

"I'm sorry I took Patches, Seth." His dad's eyes glimmer with sadness. "Has it been rough at home since I left?"

At his gentle tone, pain splinters Seth's chest. Silence is his usual defence. But he told Brooke everything he'd been through, and it was a huge relief. *How much harder can it be to tell Dad?*

Before he can begin, the waitress arrives with plates of bacon, eggs, hash browns, and toast. Seth's hunger overpowers his queasiness, and he digs into his food.

In a few minutes, his dad tries again. "You can tell me the truth, son."

This time, Seth seizes the chance and opens up. About Bert, about Keith, about his mom. When he lifts his gaze, his dad is listening hard, his face frozen. He hasn't touched his food. Seth goes quiet.

His dad watches him, then lifts his hand and beckons him on. "Keep going, Seth, it's all right."

But Seth has said enough for now. He tickles Patches behind the ears.

His dad's phone rings. He checks the call display, clenches his jaw, and presses a button. "Yeah." His face tightens. Seth thinks he can hear his mom's voice. "He's with me." The voice rants, and Seth's dad holds the phone a foot away from his ear. After a while, he brings the receiver close to his mouth. "We'll talk later." He ends the call.

The waitress stops by and eyes the full plate in front of Seth's dad. "Is there a problem with the food?"

He waves his hand. "Not at all. Just taking my time."

When the waitress moves away, he opens his mouth to speak, then sighs and shakes his head.

"Are you okay, Dad?" Seth says finally.

"Am *I* okay? My God, Seth. I should never have taken those long-haul jobs. I left you alone with her too much." He rubs his temples. "I thought it was just her and me that were having problems. I thought things were better for you when I wasn't around." He drops his eyes to the table and shakes his head. "I'm sorry, son."

Patches whimpers, and Seth feeds him a piece of bacon. The dog gobbles it down and thumps his tail on Seth's lap.

"And as for that monster, Bert . . ." Seth's dad clenches his fists. "I'd sure like to give him a taste of his own medicine."

A glimmer of a grin plays on Seth's lips.

"But I'll do this right." He reaches across the table to squeeze Seth's shoulder. "First of all, you're coming home with me and Patches. We'll work out the rest of it from there."

In the passenger seat of the truck, Seth holds Patches on his lap. Anything he has to face will be easier with his dad's support. Knowing he can survive on his own outdoors makes him feel stronger, too. In the wild, he found shelter. He scavenged food. He made a friend. Two friends, if you count the crow that led him to the hot spring that first day. Sometimes if you take a risk, help follows.

On the side of the road stands a black-haired boy in a jean jacket, thumb outstretched.

"Dad! Slow down. Let's give him a ride."

Seth's dad lifts his eyebrows, but he shoulder-checks and pulls over.

The kid runs up to the passenger side, his brown eyes full of worry. He can't be more than twelve. Seth rolls down his window. "Where are you headed?"

"My grandma's in Helmcken Hospital. Everyone's already there."

Seth whips his head to the left. His dad is nodding, so Seth reaches around to unlock the back seat. "That's right on our way. Hop in."

# Acknowledgements

I'm grateful for the support I received at key moments during the writing of *Gone Wild*. Stephen King's *On Writing* kept me motivated as I completed the first draft. Brandi Pringle provided not only excellent company on the trail but also insight and encouragement on the page. Jane Griffith helped me find a way out of an impasse. Kat Mototsune's editorial acumen challenged me to refine the narrative. A professional development leave made possible by the Camosun College Faculty Association allowed me precious time to focus on the manuscript. The Juan de Fuca Marine Trail itself both inspired this novel and grounds it, and I thank the Pacheedaht and T'Sou-ke First Nations for sharing their traditional territory with backpackers like myself.